FAERIE FOLK:

Aine Volume 2

Kathleen S. Allen

FAERIE FOLK:
Aine 2

Copyright © 2011 by Kathleen S. Allen

Printed in the United States of America
ISBN-13: 978-1461146971
ISBN-10: 1461146976

For
All those who believe in
faeries

FAERIE FOLK:
Aine 2

Jess and Sarah hugged her. She laughed at their banner: WELCOME HOME FROM IRELAND AINE!. Sarah blushed as she rolled it up so it wouldn't tear.

"I mean it, thanks you guys. It's sweet of you." Aine hooked an arm around Jess leaning into her.

"Let's go, Aine," her mom said coming up behind them carrying Aine's luggage.

"Oh, sorry, Mom. Can Jess and Sarah come with us? Please?" She crossed her fingers for luck.

Her mom smiled. "Sure, why not. I think a stop at Starbucks is in order, don't you?" All three of the girls squealed.

After they had gotten their coffees and sat down, Aine's mom held her laptop she always carried with her under her arm. "You girls hang out for a bit, I've got some work to catch up on. Let me know when you're ready to go." She gave them a wave as she set up at another table. Aine waited until her mom appeared engrossed in her work before leaning in to whisper.

"I'm getting married," she said smiling.

"What? When? You're only sixteen!" Jess said in a loud voice. Aine shushed her glancing at her mom. Her mom engrossed in her computer work did not look up.

"My mom doesn't know yet."

"Is it the guy you met on the plane? Patrick?" Sarah wanted to know.

"Yes, and we aren't getting married until after graduation. Mine, not his."

"Tell us about him," Jess said scooting her chair closer to Aine's.

"Well, he's Irish and he's a senior at Harvard."

"A senior? You mean he's in college?" Sarah's eyes widened. "He's too old for you Aine."

Aine laughed. "Let me finish Sarah. Well, he's actually a graduate student finishing his Master's in Irish Studies but in the fall he's going to med school. When I graduate we will plan a ceremony on the beach near my Great Aunt's cottage in Ireland." Aine took a sip of her coffee. "She left it to me in her will. Well, it was really a letter but still."

"She died?" Sarah said turning pale. "What happened?"

"It started with pneumonia but it weakened her heart. Even though I was only there for a few months, I loved her like I loved Granny Kate."

"I am sorry she died too," Jess said. Sarah nodded. The two of them were so opposite Aine couldn't imagine how they became friends. Sarah, a slight blonde who is shy and has a tendency to blush and Jess, a dark haired girl with flashing dark eyes who has an opinion about everything. She is not shy. Aine smiled at her two best friends.

"Tell me what's been going on here?" Aine looked from one to the other.

"Will the school let you finish the tenth grade?" Sarah asked. "You've missed so much," she worried.

"I was homeschooled while I was in Ireland so I should be okay," Aine said.

"What if they make you take tenth grade again?" Sarah asked biting on a nail.

"Will you stop bothering Aine so much, you give me a headache," Jess said. Sarah blushed again.

"I'm wondering if you'll be at school on Monday or not," Sarah said.

"I plan on it," Aine said. "Unless you know different?" She looked at one then the other. Both girls shook their heads. "Great, Monday it is."

"Will you go to the spring dance?" Sarah asked ducking her head and taking a sip of her latte.

"I doubt it, when is it?" Aine asked. She looked at Jess who rolled her eyes and mouthed, "Ask her."

"You going, Sarah?" Aine asked.

Sarah smiled. "Yes, that cute guy in my chemistry class asked me. His name is Chad."

"Great name," Aine said smiling. She looked at Jess but before she could ask anything Jess shook her head.

"Don't bother to ask me, I would not be caught dead going to a stupid high school dance," Jess said. Aine knew if someone asked her she'd go.

"We can hang out together since I'm not going either. We can watch a couple of movies, do popcorn, eat junk food until we throw up!" Aine said. Jess laughed.

"It's a plan," she said smiling. Sarah looked hurt as if they would deliberately get together without her.

"And when you get home from the dance if you aren't too tired you can come over and tell us all about Chad," Aine said trying to get Sarah to smile. It worked. A huge smile crept across her face.

"Thanks. The dance is in two weeks. Can you guys help me find a dress? It's semi-formal and I have no idea what semi-formal means."

"It means expensive," Jess joked.

Aine held up her coffee cup. "To the mall!" she said with a salute.

"The mall!" The other two did the same thing all three of them collapsing with laughter.

Aine unpacked before going down to supper. She wasn't hungry. The coffee filled her up too much. She stared at her phone then shrugged. Her mom told her she could call Patrick anytime she wanted. She punched in his number. He answered right away.

"Hello?"

"It's me," Aine said smiling. She had almost forgotten his lovely Irish brogue.

"Where are you?" he asked.

"Home in Michigan. Are you back at Cambridge yet?"

"Nope, still in Galway. My Ma has some jobs for me to do on the house before I head back to school. My flight leaves on Tuesday." He hesitated. "She wants to meet you, Aine. She won't fly, she's afraid of flying. Want to come to Galway this summer? I know I promised I'd come visit you in Michigan but..." his voice trailed off.

"I'll have to ask my mother. I don't know if we can afford another trip there so soon."

"I'll pay for the ticket, Aine."

"I didn't mean you had to...I mean..." *What did I mean?* Ireland seemed so far away now. The whole banshee thing was almost like a dream. *I am a banshee.* An Irish fairy who keens or sings for sick or dying family members of the first Irish families. In Aine's case it was the Kavannah's and their descendents. She found out she was a banshee on her 16th birthday and since then she has keened for her Granny Kate and for her Great Aunt

Ginny Ma both of whom died. But she hadn't keened for anyone else since Christmas. *Would it even work in America?* she wondered. Patrick said something.

"I'm sorry, what?"

"I said talk to your mother and if she says yes, text me some dates. I'll need them in advance so I can get a good price on a flight. Oh, how long do you want to stay? Is two weeks too long? We could explore the Irish countryside. There are some great places to see here."

"I..er..I'll have to let you know." She heard her mom calling her from downstairs. "I better go Patrick, I hear my mom calling me to come and eat supper."

He laughed. "I forgot about the time difference, its morning here, early morning."

"Did I wake you? I'm sorry."

"Its fine, I am awake. I'll call you next time. I love you, Aine."

"I love you too," she said flipping her phone to OFF. She stood in her room staring at the mirrored reflection of herself. She saw a small girl with wild curly reddish coloured hair sticking out in all directions, green eyes, freckles dusted on her pert nose and a pointed chin. She examined her ears. The elongated tips made her look more like a faerie. She lifted her shirt and stared at the tiny birthmark of a tiny pair of wings below her right shoulder.. *The banshee mark.* She pulled her shirt down. She threw her chest out trying to make her breasts look bigger. It was no use. They were small like the rest of her.

"Aine! Dinner!"

"Coming, Mom," she called tossing her phone on the bed. She didn't want to think of Patrick right now. She wasn't sure she wanted a serious boyfriend much less be engaged. Two years. A lot can change in two years. "Maybe I'll have breasts by then," she said aloud to the empty room as she sprinted down the stairs. *Maybe not.*

It was as if she never left. Except this was sophomore year instead of freshman year. The teachers piled on the homework, the same people hifived her, the same ones ignored her, Jess and Sarah stuck to her like glue. She was the different one.

Lunch was a hurry-up affair, twenty minutes to go through the line, find a table, sit down, and eat before the second warning bell rang. Aine dawdled over her salad. She

11

didn't feel like eating. She didn't fit in here. Not anymore.

Jess noticed. "What's wrong with you? Not enjoying your first day?"

"No, it's just that…" How could she tell them she wasn't like them? A normal teenage girl with crushes on the cute boys, going shopping, dreaming of college, planning a future? Her future was planned. All of it. She toyed with her lettuce some more.

"Out with it, you've been out of it since you got back," Jess said taking a bite of her burger.

"Oh, you mean since three days ago?" Aine asked.

"Yeah and before, something's changed, tell me what's wrong," Jess said around mouthfuls of her hamburger. She washed them down with a sip of her Coke.

Aine looked around at the crowded cafeteria. "Not here. Not now. After school. Can I come to your place?"

"Sorry, I've got flute lessons and then I have to babysit the Brat." The Brat was Jess' little brother. "Can't you tell me now? Is it about the Irish boy?"

"Leave her alone Jess, she said she didn't want to tell you right now," Sarah said standing up to throw her tray away in the nearest trash receptacle.

"Fine, call me later and we can chat or email me." The warning bell rang. The three of them went to their respective afternoon classes. Sarah walked with Aine to her English Literature class.

"You are so lucky to be in English Lit with Chad, " Sarah said looking in the doorway and waving to a blond boy who waved back. "He's in my chemistry lab but we aren't lab partners."

"Oh, that's Chad?"

"Yes, that's Chad. I better go. Call me too or text me." Aine nodded. She had to talk to someone about this…this…gift wasn't the right word for it. More like burden. She handed the English teacher her slip. He indicated an empty seat. She sank into her seat just as the last bell rang. *How am I supposed to get through this?*

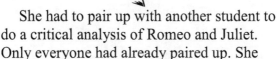

She had to pair up with another student to do a critical analysis of Romeo and Juliet. Only everyone had already paired up. She sighed. A pair of legs stood next to her desk.

"Need a partner?" Chad asked smiling down at her.

"You don't have one?" Aine asked. "I thought Mrs. Mahoney assigned them last week."

"I was out sick. I guess you were too." *Yeah, something like that.*

"Sure, grab a chair." He sat down opening his book. "I'm Aine, it," Its pronounced Annie but it's spelled Aine," she explained.

"I'm Chad. And its pronounced like its spelled. C.H.A.D." he grinned. "I saw you talking to Sarah, you know her?"

"We went to kindergarten together and first grade and second grade…well, you get the picture."

He grinned at her again. His mouth sort of went lopsided when he smiled. His blue eyes twinkled. His mop of blond hair threatened to obscure his vision every time he moved his head. *No wonder Sarah likes him*, Aine thought. *He's cute.*

"Now, what do you know about this play?" he asked. "Have you read it?"

"I have. Several times."

He smiled. "Great, because I can't figure out this language at all. I watched the

14

Leonardo movie and then I tried to read the play. Where is the gun? Does Romeo have it?" Aine sighed. *This will be a long project.*

After class Chad walked her to her locker talking about the play. Sarah fiddled with her locker.

"Hey, Chad," Sarah said blushing and tucking a strand of hair behind one ear.

"Hey yourself Sarah, what's up?"

"Nothing. I see you met my friend Aine. What are you two doing?" Aine tried the locker combination, she spun the dial several times and her three numbers but it still wouldn't open. 32, 44, spin twice around then 2. Nope, nothing.

"Damn thing," she muttered clanging the lock against the locker.

"Language young lady," said a teacher hurrying by.

"Want me to help?" Chad asked.

"Sure, why not. The combo is 32, 44 and 2. But it's no use, it won't open," Aine said. Sarah stood off to one side frowning. *At me?*

Chad got it open the first time. He beamed at her. "Got it, here you go."

"Thanks, you must have magic fingers," she said. *What a stupid thing to say!* The warning bell rang. "Oh, better go, thanks again Chat. See ya Sarah." She grabbed her math book and took off at a run. She glanced behind her. Sarah still stood staring at her. Chad had a huge grin on his face. *I think he likes me. Poor Sarah.*

She did her math homework first because it was her least favorite class. She saved English for last, her reward for making it through the math. Concentrating on Shakespeare she didn't notice when her mom poked her head in from the doorway.

"Busy?" her mom asked.

"No, come in, I'm trying to weed through Romeo and Juliet, again."

Her mom came in and sat on the bed. "How was your day?"

"Fine, it was almost as if I I was still in ninth grade. Except…" She hesitated.

"Except?"

"Except I feel different than I did. Like I don't fit in anymore."

"Give it some time; you've been away since last year. Are you sure you can handle the work in order to pass sophomore year?"

"Yes, I think so. I don't want to be behind Jess and Sarah. I want to graduate with my class."

"Okay, but if you get too overwhelmed I can get you a tutor or you can go to summer school."

Aine hesitated. "Speaking of summer, Patrick wants me to come to Galway for a couple of weeks to meet his mother this summer."

"Oh?"

"Mom, don't 'oh' me," Aine said in exasperation.

"What do you want to do?"

"I don't know." Aine gathered up her hair and twisted it into a ponytail. She took a tie from her nightstand and put it around her hair. She stalled. "I don't know. On the one hand I'd love to go to Ireland again and he said he'd buy the ticket so no money worries."

"And on the other hand?" her mom asked.

"I don't know if I want a serious relationship right now. I mean I'm only sixteen and he is my first boyfriend. I don't know if I want to be engaged to be married. I haven't even been to a high school dance yet!" She flopped back on the bed.

"You know I want you to make your own decisions Aine. But you have to go with

17

your gut feelings on this. If you think Patrick is not the right boy for you then he probably isn't."

"I think he is the right boy for me. Someday." Should she tell her mom about the vision she had of him as a doctor handing her a red-haired baby? *No. Not now.*

"I think it's a good idea to not get too serious right now," her mom said. "You'll have plenty of time for dating after college, or maybe when you are forty." Aine laughed along with her mom.

"Thanks Mom, is dinner ready?"

"Yes, that's why I came up here in the first place. I made your favourite."

"French toast?"

"No, Irish stew!" Aine shook her head. Her mom was too funny. Smiling she went down the stairs.

2

Chad called to set up a time they could work on the play together. Aine had a sinking feeling that Sarah would not approve.

"I'll get back to you Chad, I'm super busy right now trying to catch up." The truth was she didn't want Sarah to be mad at her.

"No problem, Aine. I'll see you in class. I guess Mrs. M. will let us have some class time to work on it." He hesitated. "Are you going to the Spring dance next week?"

"No, why?"

"I thought that if you were going you might save me a dance." *Uh-uh, no, nope.*

"Sorry, I have plans." She hung up before he could say more. *Why me? Is it this banshee thing that attracts guys?*

Her phone rang in her hand. She almost didn't answer it thinking it was Chad again. She looked at the number. *Sarah.*

"Hi Sarah."

"Hi Aine. I…er…wanted to talk to you about something."

"Me too. Can you come over?"

"No, I can't. I wanted to ask you something," Sarah said.

"Go ahead."

"Do you like Chad? I mean, you know, like-like him?"

"No, not at all, why?" Aine sighed.

"It's just that I got this vibe from the two of you at school. And all he does is talk about you whenever we're together. He thinks you are smart."

Aine laughed. "Yeah, Sarah we're in love and running away together." Silence on the other end told Aine she'd gone too far. "Look Sarah, he's your guy not mine. We are doing a project in English together, that's it. I promise you."

"So, you're not interested in him?"

Aine sighed again. "No, Sarah I am not interested in him."

"Well, that's a relief." Aine could hear the smile in Sarah's voice. "Now what did you want to tell me?"

"Nothing, I wanted to tell you about the project, that's all."

"Okay, thanks. See ya later." Sarah hung up. Aine hung up too. She stared at the phone before putting it down on the dresser.

Not only did she lie to her best friend but she still had no one to talk to about this whole faerie thing. She wished she still had her Granny Kate here to talk to. She was the one that told her about the banshee legend on her 16th birthday. She gave Aine a green silk dress that her great-grandmother had given her on her 16th birthday. A birthmark of a pair of tiny wings on the back of her right shoulder indicated she had the gift that ran in her family. The gift of being a banshee. And her children's children would get the gift. A female child. If she had children. In Ireland she could sing to the seals and sang when Granny Kate died soon after she got to Ireland. She didn't believe it at first. A banshee? She thought she was sad, so sad she had to sing about her sorrow. When Great Aunt Ginny Ma died right after Christmas she knew she sang again. This time she knew she was a banshee. Everyone, including her cousin Claire told her she was the designated one. The chosen one. The one with the special birthmark on her shoulder. A faerie. She had no choice but to sing for Ginny Ma. Seven days and seven nights of exhausting singing for all hours. Collapsing afterwards with Patrick to soothe her with peppermint tea. He was a faerie too. Or he said he was one. His grandmother had been a Silkie, a half-human/half-seal. But he wasn't a true Silkie, the most he could do was call to the seals. And what about me? *What can I do besides sing for the dead and dying?*

The days dragged by. On the night of the dance she called Jess.

"I'm begging off on tonight, Jess. I have a monster of a headache."

"You sure? You should see Sarah's dress, it's gorgeous. She sent you a pix on your phone."

Aine sighed. She didn't help Sarah pick out the dress like she promised. "So, you helped her find a dress?"

"Yeah, her mom and I."

"I'm sorry, I forgot all about going shopping."

"It's okay, we know you're trying to catch up on your school stuff. Look I better go and help Sarah with her hair. Text me later." She hung up. Aine sighed again. She was a bad friend.

Aine went downstairs. Her mom sat on the sofa reading. "Mom? Can I take the car to Jess's house?"

"Sure, be careful you haven't driven in the dark very much." At least she finally had her driver's license.

"It's only a couple of blocks from here. I'm going to help Sarah get ready for the dance tonight."

"You're not going?"

"No, Jess and I are going to watch a movie instead."

"Make sure you're home by twelve," her mom said going back to her book.

"I will, thanks, mom." Aine's steps lightened as she walked to the car. It was still a thrill to get into the car and start the engine. She drove to Jess's house and parked outside. She stayed in the car considering her options. Another car pulled into the driveway and Chad got out. He strode up to the door. A porch light illuminated him. He looked good in his tux. But he must be cold without a coat on. Almost as if he felt her eyes on her he turned to stare at the car. He ducked his head to see who was inside. She slid down in her seat but, he saw her. She pasted a smile on her face as he approached the car.She rolled the window down as he got closer.

"Hi, Aine, what are you doing here?"

"I came over to help Sarah get ready for the dance but I'm too late, guess she's ready. Jess and I are going to watch a movie." He leaned into her window. She thought he wanted to kiss her so she backed away from him. But instead he smiled.

"Come with us to the dance, Aine. You owe me a dance for the 'A' we got on our English paper."

"I'm not exactly dressed for a semi-formal and if I remember correctly I did most of the work on the paper."

He grinned again. "Yeah, well. Come anyway."

"No, Chad, I can't."

"At least come out on a date with me?" She hesitated. She liked Chad. A lot. But so did Sarah.

"Aren't you dating Sarah? As in one of my best friends Sarah?"

"No, we're only going to the dance together, we aren't dating." *Not the way Sarah talked.*

She shrugged. "I don't know Chad. Maybe. You better go, Sarah's waiting."

Sarah stood on the porch alongside Jess. Both of them stared at her. Chad walked over to Sarah. Aine had no choice but to get out of the car. She walked to the porch, her coat flapping. She had forgotten to button it.

"Sarah, I love your hair," Aine said. Sarah (or Jess) had piled Sarah's hair on top of her head in loose curls. "Show me your dress." Sarah opened her coat. She wore a pale blue dress that floated around her knees. "Pretty," Aine said smiling. Neither Sarah or Jess had said a word yet. Chad handed Sarah a small box.

"Here is your flower my lady," he joked. Sarah took the orchid but made no move to pin it on her dress. Chad hesitated not sure what he should do.

"You're supposed to pin it on. Want me to do it?" Chad asked. He took the box from her fingers. He fumbled with the box before taking the flower out. He blew on his fingers. The winter cold seeped into the skin. In spite of the calendar saying it was spring, winter refused to let go. Chad didn't seem to realize that Sarah stood silent. He pinned on the flower and stepped back to admire his handiwork.

"Looks great, we better go, nice seeing you, Jess. Aine." He took Sarah's elbow steering her toward his car. As soon as they were inside the car. Aine turned to Jess.

"My head is better so I guess we can do the movie thing after all." She buttoned her coat against the cold. "Can we go in? It's freezing out here."

Jess glared at her. "You seriously think I want to invite you in after what you just did?"

Aine looked confused. "Did? What did I do?"

"You know what you did, Aine. Flirting with Chad? Hello! We saw you laughing with him, the way he was leaning in the car. Did he kiss you? Sarah told me how much you've monopolized his time over the past couple of weeks. You have a boyfriend, remember? Leave Sarah's alone!"

"In the first place Chad is not her boyfriend. He only asked her out on one date. One date does not make a boyfriend." Aine ticked off her points on her finger. Her frozen fingers. "In the second place I have no control over what Chad does or doesn't do. Third, we were working on a class project, a CLASS project for the past two weeks. We sort of had to spend time together. And last, he doesn't want to be her boyfriend. He asked me out on a date tonight."

"And you think that redeems you?" Jess asked. "Sarah likes him, Aine. Leave him alone for her sake."

"I am not doing anything!" Aine said.

"You don't have to do anything, haven't you seen the way the boys look at you? Ever since you came back from Ireland you have this air about you. I can't figure it out but as soon as the guys in my classes find out I'm your friend they want to know who you are dating and if they have a chance with you. I'm sick of it! Leave Chad alone, I mean it!" She trounced back into her house and slammed the door in Aine's face.

"Fine!" Aine shouted. She kept it together until she got to the car. Then she burst into tears. *I wish I had never left Ireland!* She lay her head on the steering wheel. An emptiness inside her welled up threatening to consume her. She swallowed hard against the bile in her throat. She drove around for while reluctant to go home and face her mom. She ended up at a coffee shop that stayed open late on Friday nights. She got herself a latte and sat down staring at the darkness outside.

"This seat taken?" said a voice. She dragged her eyes upwards. A man with dark hair and eyes smiled down at her. He looked familiar but she couldn't place him.

"No, feel free." She thought he wanted the extra chair instead he sat down across from her blowing on his cup before taking a sip.

"I...er...I'm not in the mood for company," she said. She might as well have a sign on her forehead that read: FAERIE HERE.

"I'm not going to bother you Aine."

"Aine? You know my name?" He used the Irish pronunciation, An-Yah rather than Annie, which is how she pronounced it.

"Yes."

She waited. "How do you know me?"she asked.

"I know your family. I am a friend of your cousin Claire. She told me to look you up when I came back to school." He took another sip of his coffee. "I called your house and your ma told me you went out. I came here to get a coffee and here you are."

28

"How did you know it was me?" Aine asked taking a sip of her coffee. *Good.* "This is a good latte." He nodded.

"Your cousin described you to me. You are easy to find with that hair you know."

She laughed. "I know."

"Plus the whole faerie thing you have going on. It's like a magnet, it draws me in."

She choked on her last drink of coffee. "What are you talking about?" she asked feigning innocence.

He chuckled. "I am a faerie too, Aine. My name is Fennen and I am your faerie protector. I'm here to help you." He smiled.

"Help me do what?"

He smiled. She had acknowledged she would listen to him. She frowned.

"I am here to protect you from Grianne."

"What do you mean? Protect me from who?" Aine took another sip of her coffee. She looked around the room but no one paid any attention to them. She relaxed a little.

"Grianne is a dark faerie. She is evil. She plots to destroy your magic. She wants to steal the Queen's crown so she will be Queen of both the dark and the light lands of the faeries. If that happens, she will kill off the land of the light faeries. And evil will reign over the earth. The faeries will no longer be able to help the humans."

"Help the humans? Do what?"

"The Selchies help the fishing industry and so do the Mer-people. The Wood-Elves help the forests to flourish, the Kelpie's help the oceans along with the pixies. The Peri's help the humans do good deeds. The Sylph's give them creativity." He sighed. "We do so many things for the humans they do not know about." He looked at her. "All of those and more would be gone if Grianne is allowed to destroy us."

"Where is this Grianne now?"

"Here."

"Here as in this coffee shop?" Aine looked around but none of the other patrons looked scary enough to be a dark faerie goddess. "What does she look like?" She had her eye on a possible candidate hiding in the corner with her laptop open but not appearing to do any work. She caught Aine's eye and stared at her. Aine looked back at Fennen.

He laughed. "No, here in America. We just aren't sure where yet. As for looks, she looks ordinary, like you or me. But make no mistake, she is after you and she means to destroy you."

"Seriously?" Aine's eyes grew wide.

"Yes. This is serious." She looked at him.

"You off your medications?" she asked. "Do you hear Elvis talking to you?"

He laughed again. "Nice Buffy reference but no. I am sent by the CIF. I am one of their agents."

"The CIF? Like the FBI?"

"Sort of. More like INTERPOL. I belong to The Council of International Faerie or CIF. We protect all the classes of faerie."

"So, you're a banshee too?"

"No, I am not. Only females can be banshees. I am just an ordinary faerie."

Aine smiled as if those words could be used together in a sentence. "And what about Patrick Sullivan, do you know him?"

"Of course I do. We are good friends. His grandmother was a Silkie, male Selchies are rare though." He smiled. "I used the Irish pronunciation of it. It's spelled S E L C H I E. Do you know that the only way a human mortal can have a male Selchie's child is to cry seven tears into the sea or seven drops of blood? Then after seven years he claims the

31

child as his own and she is no longer needed."

"Sounds like a typical man, leave the woman to raise the kid then want them back just when they get interesting." He ignored her comment.

"How many classes of faerie are there?" she asked.

"Fifteen recognized by the CIF. Those are the Sidhe."

"Sidhe?"

"Faerie folk." He took a last sip of his coffee before getting up. "Of course there are sub-classes of each one too." He grinned. "I'll be in touch, Aine. Stay safe. Let me know if you see Grianne."

"How will I know if I see her?"

"Oh, you'll know. Here's my card, it has my email, mobile phone, Twitter and office numbers on it. The X11 is the emergency CIF number. Call that one any time you are in danger. But I'll be around too. I'm your protection."

"Wait; is my mom in danger too?"

He nodded. "Yes, of course she is. Everyone is in danger as long as Grianne is around."

"But, how do I stop her?"

"You don't. I will stop her. She's s type of banshee called a Korrigan. She seduces mortal men and then kills them." He looked at his phone. "I gotta go Aine. I'll be in touch."

He left. Aine finished her coffee and left too.

As luck would have it her mom was in bed so she didn't have to explain her evening to her. Not that she could explain it anyway. Between the fight with Jess, Sarah's coolness, Chad's asking her out and the strange guy at Starbucks she would have a hard time explaining any of it. She checked and double-checked the locks on the windows and the doors. Not that a lock would keep out a faerie. She wondered if garlic did anything to faeries? She laughed at herself. She ate garlic all the time and it didn't bother her. She was a faerie too. Wasn't she? She got ready for bed. Just before climbing under the covers she glanced at her phone. A Voice Mail from Patrick.

"Hi, Aine, back at Cambridge. Guess who transferred here? Claire. She's going to Harvard Law. She says to tell you hi. Well, goodnight, Aine. I just wanted to tell you that I love you. Call me or text me when you get a chance. Love you."

Aine shut the phone off. Claire was in Cambridge? *What is she doing in Cambridge?*

3

Aine spent the weekend doing household chores. Catching up on laundry, helping her mom clean, finishing up homework. She picked up her phone several times to call Jess or Sarah but put it down each time. *They don't want to hear from me.* She hoped Sarah would call to tell her about the dance but her phone remained silent.

She called Patrick instead. She wanted to ask him about this new guy she met.

"Yeah?" he asked.

"Hi Patrick, it's Aine." *Or should I say An-Yah?*

"I got your message. I'm glad you made it back okay. You said Claire is there too?"

"Yes, in fact she's here right now. Want to talk to her?"

"Sure, I guess I…" But before she could finish Claire came on the line.

"Hey An, what's up? How's tenth grade?"

"Fine. What are you doing there, Claire?" Aine couldn't help feeling a tiny bit jealous that her cousin Claire who used to go to Columbia Law School in New York City was now at Harvard with Patrick.

"I transferred. I wanted to be closer to family," Claire snapped her gum in Aine's ear.

"What family?"

"Patrick of course. As soon as you get married he'll be my cousin once removed by marriage or something," she laughed. "Anyway, I was tired of NYC. I like Boston better."

"What about Greg?"

"Greg who?"

"The guy you went skiing with over Christmas break?" *The guy who was so important you missed Ginny Ma's last Christmas? That guy.*

"Oh, yeah, him. We broke up. I am on the prowl for a new boyfriend now," she said. "Isn't that right Patrick darling?" The way she said Patrick's name made Aine's teeth grind together. Claire flirted with every boy she met. Including Patrick. Aine seethed with jealousy.

"Put Patrick back on," Aine said.

"Okay, see ya cuz."

"Hello?" Patrick said. "Did you ask your mom about coming to Ireland this summer?"

"I did but she hasn't given me an answer yet."

"Keep me posted babe."

"I will. Oh, I got my driver's license finally."

"Great. Any other news?"

"Er...no, not really." Nothing except a dark faerie named Grianne is after me and my family. My best friends hate me. My best friend's date is hitting on me and I met my faerie protector in Starbucks last night. *No, nothing new.*

Aine knew that school would be complicated on Monday morning. She usually got dropped off early so she could meet Jess and Sarah in the cafeteria for breakfast. This morning she scanned the tables. No Jess. No Sarah. She got her oatmeal and OJ. She sprinkled on the brown sugar before pouring a bit of cream into the bowl. She sampled a bite. She added another teaspoon of sugar. She put a spoonful in her mouth. *Better.* Chad plopped down on the seat across from her a big grin on his face.

"Hey, Aine." She nodded at him swallowing.

"Chad." She pointed to the empty place in front of him. "Where's your breakfast?"

"I ate at home. Sarah told me you usually eat breakfast at school so here I am."

"Where is Sarah?"Aine asked.

"I dunno. I haven't seen her since the dance Saturday night."

"Did you have fun at least?" Aine asked taking another bite of her oatmeal.

"Yep. Ready for our date Friday night?" He beamed at her. She sighed.

"About that Chad. See, Sarah really likes you and I don't want to hurt her feelings so…"

He interrupted her. "It's not like Sarah and I are boyfriend and girlfriend we just went to the dance and made out afterwards. No big deal."

"Made out afterwards?" Aine stopped reaching for the OJ her hand frozen in mid-air.

"Yeah, you know. A hook up, nothing more." He shrugged. *This is bad!*

Aine shook her head. "No, thanks Chad. I mean it. I'm not going out with you. Find someone else to bug."

"Fine but if you change your mind…"

"I won't." Sarah and Jess chose that moment to walk into the cafeteria. Sarah spotted them immediately. She led Jess over to the table a scowl on her face directed at Aine.

"Isn't this a cozy picture?" Jess asked staring at Chad.

"'Lo ladies, I am leaving. See you in class, Aine. Sarah. Jess." He took off on a run. *Coward.*

"What is going on with you and Chad?" Sarah asked watching Chad bolt out the door. She turned back to Aine.

"Nothing, he was telling me about the dance."

"Oh? He told you I lost my virginity to him?" *It's worse than I thought.*

"No, he said he had fun, that's all. Sit down Sarah, we can talk about it."

"Why would I sit down with the girl who wants to steal my boyfriend?" Aine sighed.

"You might want to talk to Chad about that. He doesn't think you are even dating at this point."

"Oh, really? Did you agree to go out with him?" Jess wanted to know.

"No, I…well, I did at first but I told him I couldn't now because…"

"You are a horrible person," Sarah said tears in her eyes. "You know how much he means to me and you…you…" She ran out of the room sobbing. Aine looked at her retreating back then at Jess who stood next to the table.

"Oh, sit down Jess, please. Let me explain."

"I think the time for explaining is over Aine. You've changed since you were in Ireland. And not for the better I might add. I don't think I want to be friends with you anymore." She whipped around heading out the door before Aine could respond. *Could this day get any worse?*

Aine managed to make it through the day without annoying anyone else. Chad sent her love notes in English Lit in badly written Shakespeare.

> Forsooth, Thine eyes are like two lipid---she hoped he meant liquid---pools of greenness surrounded by a face as lovely as can be. Your lips are red, like the red, red, rubies and

so is your hair. Go out with me!
Your knight in English Lit, Chad

She laughed folding it up and sticking it
in her bookbag. She looked over at him and
mouthed the word, "NO." But her smile
gave her away. What harm would it do to go
out with an ordinary boy? A boy who knew
nothing about her faerie life? A boy whose
only mission in life was to "hook up?" She
turned back around and nodded to him. He
gave her a thumbs up.

The bell rang and the hordes of students
trying to escape shoved Aine toward the
general vicinity of her locker. Once she was
near it she stood her ground until the pack
dissipated. She sighed staring at the
combination lock. It befuddled her. A hand
reached out spun the dial once, then twice
and the lock clicked open. Chad smiled at
her.

"It's all in the wrist you know. So, you'll
go out with me?" He looked so hopeful.

"I said I would. I don't want you to
breathe a word of this to anyone. Especially
not to Sarah or Jess."

"I hardly see either of them."

"Both are in your afternoon classes Chad."

"Yeah, but I don't talk to them much." He shuffled his feet back and forth. "Friday night at eight sound good? We can catch a coffee or go to the show, your choice."

"Coffee sounds great. More time to get to know each other that way."

"Good. Coffee on Friday and then on Saturday we can see a movie or just hang out. You like pizza?"

"Not really."

"Yeah? Well, burgers then?"

"Vegan, no cheese, no meat, no eggs, no diary."

His eyes opened wider. "What do you eat fruits and berries?"

"Yeah, and don't forget the twigs." She smiled wondering if that would deter him.

"That's cool." Obviously not. She put her books away, grabbing the ones she needed for that night's homework and slammed the door shut. She clicked the lock back together.

"Walk you to your car?" he asked.

"My mom drops me off, I usually take the city bus after school."

"Great, I can ride with you. I take the bus too." She found that odd since she had not seen him on the bus. She shrugged. He fell in beside her chatting about his latest video game or TV show. She wasn't really listening. She passed by Sarah and Jess waiting for their mom's to pick them up. Normally she'd ask for a ride too. Jess only lived a couple of blocks from her. But not today. *Or ever again*. She turned her head as they passed by keeping her eyes straight ahead.

"Bitch," Jess said as they walked past. Aine pretended she hadn't heard but tears stung her eyes. Chad took her hand in his swinging their arms as they walked. That small gesture comforted her.

"Mom? You home?" Aine called. The house was quiet. Aine threw her bookbag in a chair before rummaging in the 'fridge for a snack. She put together a blueberry/apple/raisin salad with a handful of walnuts. She sat down with her math homework, the salad next to her elbow.

Her cell rang. Damn. It was in her bag. She raced to get it but the phone stopped before she could answer it. She glanced at the number. *Patrick.* She took the phone to the table with her. She punched in his number.

"Hi, sorry, I couldn't get to my phone. How are you?" She settled in with her phone in one hand and a fork in the other. She was just about to take a bite of the salad.

"Why didn't you tell me you met Fennen?" he asked. She hesitated but put the food in her mouth, chewing. I admit it, I'm stalling, she thought.

"I…I didn't know what to tell you Patrick."

"You didn't think he'd call me and tell me all about Grianne? About the danger you are in? Where is he? Is he there?"

"Who Fennen? Of course he's not here. Why would he be?" A shadow out of the corner of her eye caused her to glance to the side. There stood Fennen with a grin on his face. "Oh, how stupid of me, yes, he's here. He's right here." She handed the phone to Fennen. "It's Patrick he wants to talk to you." She stabbed a piece of apple with such force it flew off her fork onto her math homework. *Great. Just great.* Fennen began to speak in Gaelic or Irish as the Irish called it. Very rapid Irish. It was hard for Aine to keep up so she gave up. She ate most of her salad by the time Fennen handed her back the phone.

"Hello?"

"I'm sorry I got angry Aine but I'm worried. Fennen says he has it covered though. No sign of Grianne yet."

"Thanks. Look Patrick I need to talk to you but not now, maybe when I AM ALONE." She emphasized the last words for Fennen's ears but he appeared to be oblivious.

"Call me later on tonight. Midnight?"

"I'll try. My mom has been getting on my case about my phone bill."

"I'll pay for your phone bill Aine. Call me tonight. I love you."

"Uh-huh," she said hanging up. She glared at Fennen who popped blueberries in his mouth like he was eating popcorn.

She waited until he finished. "Look, Fennen you can't be here when my mom gets home, she'll freak if she thinks I had a boy over when she wasn't here."

"I'm not a boy, I'm a faerie."

"Oh, that's so much better. Hey, Mom? Guess what I have a faerie who is protecting me from an evil elf."

45

"Evil faerie, not an elf." He paused. "Well, actually she's a Korrigan if you want to get technical."

"Get out of my house!" Aine yelled startling him.

"I told you, I can't. I'm protecting you."

"Well, do it from outside. I have homework to get done." She cast her eyes back down to her paper. She could feel his eyes on her. "What?" she asked without looking up.

"Can I have some more blueberries before I go?"

"Take the whole container, I'll tell mom I had a craving, just go!" He grinned taking the blueberries out of the 'fridge. He clutched the container to his chest as he sprinted out the door. Aine followed him to make sure he left. He went as far as the sidewalk then sat down eating his berries.

"Move away from there!" she yelled. He moved further down the sidewalk. At least he wasn't in front of her yard anymore.

4

She didn't want to call Patrick but she felt she owed it to him. He answered right away.

"Patrick? I wanted to talk to you."

"Sounds serious," he said.

"Look, I don't know how to say this but you know I like you. I love you. And what we had in Ireland meant so much to me. You helped me through a rough time…"

"Wow, sounds like you're breaking up with me."

"It's just that I haven't really dated anyone yet. I just got my driver's license. I'm only sixteen. I'm too young to be engaged." There, she said it. Silence greeted her. "You still there?"

"Yes, of course I am. I don't know what you want me to say to that Aine. You know we are destined to be together. Our families agreed we should be married since before either of us were born."

"What? What do you mean?"

"I wanted to tell you when you came to Ireland this summer. My parents and your Granny Kate along with Ginny Ma and your parents agreed that when we were of age we'd be mated for life. There's a contract signed by our families and ratified by the CIF."

"What? Ratified by the CIF?"

"I told you, I wanted to tell you in person." *Isn't that wonderful? Engaged to a faerie before I was even born. And a bonus, my impending marriage was ratified by the CIF.* She shook her head.

"What if we hated each other?" Aine asked.

"We wouldn't, part of the covenant is steeped in magic. We were bound together with faerie magic as infants. My fate is your fate and vice versa."

"I don't care what our parents did or didn't do Patrick, I'm too young to be engaged. Or what kind of magic we were bound with. I think I should break up with you. Don't call me again." She slammed the phone down on her bed. A knock on her door startled her.

"Aine? You okay? I heard loud voices." Her mom poked her head in.

"Did I wake you, Mom?"

"No, I happened to be in bed reading. Can I come in? Is something wrong? You look upset."

"Sure, come in. And when you do be sure and tell me all about how you and dad bound me to a boy I had never met until this past summer." Her mom had the grace to look sheepish as she sat on the bed next to her.

"Granny Kate's idea," she said smoothing the quilt on the bed with one hand as she talked.

"We knew you were a banshee as soon as you were born. You had the birthmark on your shoulder. Your dad was afraid that if you were bound to a mortal you'd lose your gift."

"You knew I was a banshee all along and never told me? Even after Ginny Ma died?" Aine felt hurt.

"I'm sorry, Aine." Her mom pronounced it the Irish way like Fennen did. "Your dad made me promise not to tell you until you were married to Patrick. I thought I had two more years. I wanted you to enjoy your last two years of high school as a mortal."

"You talk as if you are a faerie too."

49

Her mom laughed. "I am. I belong to the class of Pillywiggins."

"What is that?"

"Pillywiggins or flower faeries."

"That's why our garden flourishes even in the winter?" Aine asked.

"Yes, I have what the mortals call 'a green thumb.'"

"Why am I not a flower faerie too?"

"Your father was a mortal, we weren't sure what you'd be until you were born. I hoped you'd be a Pillywiggins too but your dad wanted you to be a mortal," she smiled at the memory. "Granny Kate was sure you'd be a banshee like she was. And sure enough, you were." All of a sudden her mom had an Irish brogue.

"Since when do you speak with an Irish brogue?" Aine asked.

"This is my natural way of speaking. The American accent is part of my faerie glamour." She looked at Aine. "Do you know what faerie glamour is?"

"The ability to make yourself seem something other than what you really are. I know how to read and look up things on the Internet, Mom."

"Just asking. Now that you know my true nature I can drop the glamour. It's exhausting to keep it up all the time." She smiled again. Aine considered what to ask next.

"What happened to my dad? You only told me he died when I was a baby."

"One of the dark faeries killed him. I put enchantments around him but they don't always work around dark faeries and mortals are especially susceptible to the dark faerie magic." She sighed. "I wanted to protect you from all that so I escaped from Ireland when you were a baby hiding my identity and yours. Granny Kate came from Ireland to help protect you as you got closer to inheriting your faerie gift."

"Was this dark faerie named Grianne?"

Her mom stared at her. "Where is he?"

"Who?"

"Fennen." And as if he heard his name called he walked into the room bowing slightly at the waist.

"I am here, Your Majesty," he said. Aine's eyes widened.

"What does he mean, Your Majesty?" Aine asked staring at her mom again.

"I am Queen Fiona O' Shea of the Pillywiggins, which makes you Princess Aine."

Aine pinched herself on the arm then said, "Ow!"

"Why did you do that?" Fennen asked.

"Trying to wake up from this nightmare," Aine said glaring at him. "Tell me again about you being Queen of the Faeries," she looked at her mom then at Fennen. "And you being a Protective Faerie and me being a banshee because a few months, a few short months ago I was obsessing about the size of my breasts and when I'd get my driver's license."

"Really? Your breasts seem fine to me," Fennen said staring at Aine's chest.

"Fennen!" Aine and her mom said at the same time. He ducked his head.

"Sorry, go on Aine," he sighed. Aine looked at him then at her mom.

"Never mind. Will the two of you get out and let me get some sleep. I do have school tomorrow you know." Her mom got up.

"Sure honey, we can talk about this more tomorrow. I'm sure you'll have lots of questions for me." She turned to Fennen. "Come on Fen, I'll make you some tea."

"'Night Aine," Fennen said waving at her from the doorway. She ignored him turning her back and pulling her covers up over her shoulder. She reached up to turn out the light. The stars shone in through her window. She thought she heard someone laughing outside but decided it was just her imagination.

Aine dragged herself to the kitchen. She threw a bagel in the toaster and poured herself a cup of tea from the kettle on the stove.

"Morning, Aine," Fennen said coming into the kitchen. He had on a clean tee shirt and low rise jeans. His feet were bare and his black hair stood up in spikes.

"So, you are sleeping here now too?" Aine said sitting down with her bagel. She spread strawberry jam lavishly on both sides. She picked up one and took a bite.

"Yes, the Queen thought it best."

"Please don't call her that." He looked puzzled.

"Why not?" He took the other half of her bagel and took a bite. "Thanks."

"I suppose you want blueberries with your bagel?" His eyes brightened.

"Are there any?"

"No, you ate them all yesterday, remember?" She felt cranky. She finished her bagel and took her tea to her room to finish getting ready for school. Her mom was still sleeping so she decided to take the bus.

Fennen waited for her on the sidewalk. He began walking next to her.

"Wait, where are you going?"

"To the bus with you then to school. Don't you have a Math quiz today?" She stopped walking.

"No way Fennen, stay home with mom or go to the mall. You are not, and I repeat myself, not going to school with me. You don't look anything like a student, you're too old."

"Ouch darlin'." He grinned at her. She spotted her bus and took off at a run. He ran next to her. She made it and so did Fennen. He took the seat next to her. She ignored him pulling out her headphones and putting on the newest single by Adam Lambert. She continued to ignore Fennen even when the bus stopped at the high school. She went straight to her locker. It wouldn't open, as usual. Fennen watched her struggle with it a

54

couple of times. He reached up and covered the lock with his hand, mumbled a few words and the lock popped open.

"How'd you...Never mind." She got out her books for the morning classes. Math was first. He followed her to her class but didn't go in. She took her seat looking over her homework to ingrain the problems into her head before the quiz.

Halfway through the quiz her math teacher tapped her on the shoulder. She blinked up at him disoriented for a moment.

"Yes?"

"Is that person with you?" He pointed to Fennen who stood in the hall staring in at them. He nodded to her with a smile on his face.

"Yes, that's my faer..er...cousin from Ireland. He wanted to come to school with me today."

"No unauthorized visitors are allowed. He has to go to the office to get a visitors badge then he can come in."

"You want me to tell him now or should I finish my quiz first?" Aine asked.

"Tell him now; I'll hold your quiz for you." *Fine.*

She went over to the door, opened it and stepped out into the hall closing the door behind her. "My teacher says you have to go to the office to get a pass before you can be here."

"Oh? Where is that? What do I have to say?"

"Tell them you are my cousin from Ireland. Do not, I repeat, do not say anything about dark faeries, banshees, the CIF or anything related. Is that clear?" she asked through gritted teeth.

He saluted her before going. She went back inside to finish her quiz. Just as she sat down the bell rang. *Of course.* She handed it in with a sigh. She heard the overhead intercom crackle.

"Will Ms. Aine O'Shea please come to the office. Ms. Aine O'Shea." *Now what?*

Fennen sat in one of the chairs. Principal Williams beckoned her into his office. She went inside and sat down.

"That your cousin from Ireland?" he asked also sitting down.

"Yes, he wanted to come to school with me to see an American high school."

"The policy is he has to be cleared ahead of time for visitors. I'm afraid I'll have to speak to your parents to verify he is your cousin. If he is your cousin, he is free to visit as long as he checks in here every morning and checks out every afternoon."

"Fine. Should he wait here? Or should I tell him to go home?"

"He can wait. I'll call your parents right now." He hit a button on his phone. "Ms. Henry? Please get Aine O'Shea's parents on the phone for me." He covered the mouthpiece with his hand. "Does your mother work?"

"Yes, but she's home today. You can call her there. Oh and by the way, my dad is dead." *Has been since I was a baby. Killed by dark faeries who are now after me.*

Fennen was approved by her mom. He got a badge and followed her to her classes. Suddenly she was very popular with the girls in her classes. Several of them swarmed around Fennen practically drooling at his Irish accent. He puffed up his chest as he reveled in the attention.

"Who's the Irish dude?" Chad asked coming up to her in the hall.

"My cousin, Fennen. He's visiting for a few days."

"Seems the ladies like him," he said.

"It's the accent, gets us every time," she laughed. He put his arms around her pulling her in close. He smelled like lemons. She sniffed him her mood lifting. The warning bell rang. She was off to Earth Science, the unit this quarter was Astronomy. Chad gave her a kiss on the cheek. Fennen frowned but ran after her as she traipsed through the students lollygagging until the last moment.

"Who is that boy who kissed you?" Fennen asked keeping up with her.

"A friend."

"What about Patrick? He's your destiny," Fennen announced. She stopped so fast he ran smack into her back. She spun around to face him.

"Let's get this straight, Fennen, Patrick is not my destiny, I can date whomever I want and I am sick of this whole thing. Go back to Ireland and leave me alone!" She took off down the hall not caring if he followed her or not.

He waited for her at home. He lounged in the living room using the remote to flip through the channels in quick secession. He smiled as she came in depositing her bookbag in the nearest empty chair. She ignored him and went to the kitchen. She poured herself a glass of iced tea. She took two cookies from the cookie jar. Yum, snickerdoodles, her favourite. Her mom must've felt guilty to do any sort of baking. She took the cookies to the table. She opened her iPhone to check her email. She saw Fennen come in but continued to ignore him.

"You gonna stay mad at me this entire time?" he asked sitting down across from her.

"Maybe."

"How 'bout I take you out to dinner tonight? You and your Ma. Show my appreciation for letting me stay here."

"Okay." She glanced up from her cookie. He grinned at her. She felt the corners of her mouth go up. "I said, Okay, didn't I?"

"Tell me about the boy kissing you," he said just as her mom walked in.

"What boy kissing you?" Her mom carried a sack of groceries. Fennen jumped up to take it from her.

"You shouldn't carry things, Your Highness, let me have that." He stood with the sack in his arms in the middle of the kitchen clearly not sure what he was supposed to do next.

"Put the groceries away," Aine said getting up to help. He put the bag down and the two of them (well, it was mostly Aine) put the groceries away. Her mom made herself a cup of tea.

"Now, what boy was kissing you?" her mom asked taking a sip of her tea.

"Chad. We're going out on Friday night. Coffee. He's just a friend Mom."

"Is he the boy who took Sarah to the dance?" her mom wanted to know.

"Yes. And please don't ask me anything else about him. Before you say anything, I am no longer engaged to Patrick. We have gone our separate ways." Aine expected a blow up but her mom surprised her.

"I think that's wise. Sixteen is too young to be engaged."

"Really?" Aine asked smiling.

"Yes, you need to live a little first. Go on dates, otherwise how will you know Patrick is the right one for you?"

Her mom didn't get it. "Patrick is not the right one Mom. We broke up. I will never see him again."

"Sure you will," Fennen piped up. "He's your des…"

"Stop saying that!" Aine said jumping up. She knocked over her tea. Horrified she watched the tea seep into the once-Ivory coloured tablecloth. It was ruined. "Mom, I am so sorry. It belonged to Granny Kate." Aine burst into tears. Her mom got up and put an arm around her shoulders.

"It's fine, Aine, it's only a tablecloth. Why don't you go to your room and get your homework done?"

"I'm taking you both out to dinner. Connor O'Neills has great Fish and Chips or so I've heard."

"Great, I've had a rough day at work," her mom said smiling at Aine. "Be ready by six?"

"Sure," Aine said wiping her face with the back of her hand. *What is the matter with me?*

I don't usually cry when I spill things. She decided it was the stress of waiting for the dark faerie to strike. Going out to dinner might take her mind off it. She relaxed and went to her room to get her homework done. That way she could enjoy dinner.

61

Tomorrow was Friday. D day. Or Date-Day, as Chad put it. She felt like they had already been on a date. They hung out at breakfast, in between classes, at lunch and after school. She found out he loved to sing, hated to write, thought science was "stupid" and all sports were "awesome." She grinned as he talked to her. They were sitting outside near the arch on a bench. They had eight minutes to get to English Lit, their last class of the day. She had her head on his shoulder and he had his arm around hers.

"This is cozy," she mumbled half-asleep.

"You smell sweet like a flower," he said sniffing her hair.

"You smell like lemons," she said. "I like it."

"Lemons? Huh. Wonder why." They both heard the bell at the same time. Aine got up.

"You know you are tiny for a girl," he said smiling down at her.

"That's only because you are over six feet tall," she said also smiling. The smile turned to a frown as she looked out over the sidewalk. Chad turned to see what she was looking at.

"Isn't that your cousin?" he asked waving at Fennen who waved back.

"Let's go," Aine said taking Chad's arm in order to steer him back to the building. He turned his neck to look at Fennen.

"Is he waiting to take the bus with you?" Chad asked.

"I don't know. I guess."

But he wasn't. When she came out of English Lit Fennen was nowhere to be seen. Chad took her hand to walk her to the bus. He usually took the bus going in the opposite direction so he only waited until her bus came. At the bus stop several students waited. Chad pulled her behind a tree and kissed her fully on the mouth. She leaned into it surprising herself.

"Wow," Chad said smiling. "You know how to kiss. I mean it. That was...wow." She grinned. She saw the bus out of the corner of her eye.

"There's my bus Chad, see you tomorrow at school."

"And don't forget tomorrow night," he grinned as she got on the bus. She looked forward to the date. Maybe she'd forget about this faerie business if only for a brief

moment. She closed her eyes letting the bus
engine lull her into a semi-doze.

5

A hand on her knee woke her up with a start.

A girl with dark curly hair but bright blue eyes smiled down at her. "I'm sorry, you moaned in your sleep, either you are having a great dream or a nightmare, which is it?"

Aine laughed. "Thanks, I think more of a nightmare. I haven't been sleeping much lately."

"Boyfriend or schoolwork?" The girl asked.

"Family stuff. I'm Aine by the way. I haven't seen you on this bus before."

"I just transferred here. Today was my first day in high school Hell."

"How'd you like it?"

"Scary but fun. I had six guys ask me out on the way to lunch!" She laughed. Her laugh was infectious, Aine laughed too.

"Are you a junior?" Aine asked. The girl had on a low cut tank top made of red silk with a red jacket over it. No wonder she got asked out. She was what the boys called "stacked." Aine blushed when she realized the girl saw her looking at her breasts.

"I…er…am admiring your necklace, its lovely."

The girl fingered it. "Thanks, it's a family heirloom. Handed down from my granny and her granny and so on." She stuck out a hand to Aine. "I'm Grace O' Malley."

"That's an Irish name if I ever heard one," Aine said. "I'm Irish-American. On my mom's side." *And a faerie.*

"My da was Irish but my Ma was from Romania. You know, gypsies? That's why I am so dark but I have my father's eyes." She laughed. "Well, not literally."

"What grade are you in?"

"Tenth."

"Me too! But I didn't see you in any of my classes, not that I would necessarily."

"I spent the entire day trying to get into classes, most of them were full. I had to have special permission and that took time. I didn't get anything I wanted except Choir third hour."

"Oh, I have Choir too. I just added it. What do you sing?"

"I don't look like it but I have a very high voice. I sing tessitura-soprano."

"Three octaves above middle C?" Aine asked.

"Yes. What about you?"

"I have no idea." *Ask the seals, they'd know.*

The bus rumbled to a stop. Aine got up. "This is my stop. I'll see you in Choir tomorrow.I'm auditioning for a spot. "

"Great, nice meeting you, Aine."

"You too."

Fennen handed her a cup of tea. He smiled at her. "How was your day?"

"Fine. Where'd you disappear to? Chad saw you standing on the sidewalk right before sixth hour. I thought you'd ride the bus with me."

"I planned on it but I got an urgent call from the CIF." He sat down sipping his tea. She sipped hers too. "I have some bad news Aine. I don't want to alarm you but Griannee has been seen in the area."

"Here? In Ann Arbor?"

"Yes. At least we think it's her. She changes her shape so often she's hard to catch. We just want you to be on guard. I'm going to go to school with you tomorrow and be your cousin again."

"I'm sure the girls will love that," Aine said frowning. "What about my date with Chad tomorrow night?"

"We'll double date. I'll ask another agent to go with us."

"No, no and no."

He crossed his arms. "Either that or you cancel it."

"Fine, but no faerie talk, I mean it."

"I get it, Chad is a mortal. Is that why you are attracted to him? I've never dated a mortal before. I never saw the need."

"I need to get my homework done," Aine said ignoring Fennen's question. She took her tea to her room and opened her Earth Science book. At least she'd have one friend besides Chad in school tomorrow. She turned to the chapter they discussed in class and started on the questions.

Chad frowned at her. "A double date? Why?"

Aine sighed. "I told you, my cousin wants to go with us. He's bringing a date. If I don't take him along I can't go either. He thinks he needs to protect me. Please, Chad? Once he goes back to Ireland we can go on a real date. Just the two of us. Alone. I promise."

He shrugged. "Whatever. I suppose. When is he going back?"

"At this point I have no idea, I hope it's soon though."

"Me too." He smiled. "Let's duck in here," he looked in the science lab. The lights were off, most of the labs didn't start until second hour. He tried the door. It was unlocked. They went inside and before Aine could step further inside Chad embraced her. He kissed her, his lips traveling from her mouth to her neck nuzzling her. She moaned. Her knees weak she backed up to the wall for support, Chad following her. Aine felt dizzy. Chad's hands explored under her blouse. Black spots in front of her eyes made her breathe faster. She pushed Chad off of her, his mouth still seeking hers.

"Stop, Chad, we have to get to class."

"I want you, Aine," he said his voice husky with longing.

"I want you too Chad but not here in school. Let's go." She straightened her blouse. *What am I doing?* "I'll see you at lunch." She ran out the door before he could answer. Her head still swimming from the emotions she experienced. She ran smack into Sarah who had been balancing a load of books in her arms. The books scattered all over the floor.

"Damn it," Sarah said glaring at Aine. "Watch where you are going, O'Shea."

"I'm sorry, Sarah I didn't see you." Aine scrambled to help Sarah pick up the books. Both of them heard the warning bell at the same time.

"Now I'm going to be late," Sarah grumbled. Aine handed her the last book.

"Here you go, I'm sorry I made you late." She smiled but Sarah did not return the smile. She took off down the hall at a clip. *Will Sarah ever forgive me?*

"Who was that?" A voice asked. Aine turned to see the new girl, Grace standing there.

"Sarah Turnsdale, she's my…I mean she used to be one of my…never mind. Where you headed?"

"Earth Science with Mr. Collins. You?"

"Same, let's go. He never starts on time though so I doubt we'll have missed anything."

The choir teacher, Ms. Tilda asked Grace
to sing a few notes in order to place her in
the right section. Ms. Tilda started at middle
C and kept going. When she reached the
high G above high C she stopped. Grace
smiled.

"Well, I see you are right, Ms. O'Malley,
you are a tessitura. Stand with the soprano's.
Aine? I believe you are next. Come to the
front please." Aine stepped down the risers
to the front. Mrs. Tilda hit a note on the
piano. She ran up the scales once. "See if
you can sing any of these notes." She played
one. Aine sang out loud and clear. Mrs.
Tilda kept going, so did Aine. She played
the high G above middle C and Aine sang
that too. Mrs. Tilda looked stunned. "Why
didn't you tell me you could sing tessitura.
It's unusual to have two tessitura-soprano's
in the same choir but, it's a good kind of
unusual. Can you sing this piece?" She
handed Aine some sheet music. It was a
song in Latin. Aine began to sing. She
closed her eyes to get the full effect of the
song raising her voice so that it rang out
echoing.

"Stop!" several girls cried. Aine stopped
singing and opened her eyes. All of the girls

71

in the choir were crying, and so were some of the boys. Grace grimaced holding her hands over her ears as if she were in pain.

"That's enough, Aine," Mrs. Tilda said wiping away a tear. "Your singing makes me," she indicated the rest of the choir with a sweep of her hand, "and everyone else sad when you sing. "Take a seat." Aine was regulated to the chairs the tone-deaf students sat in. They spent the hour doing their homework instead of singing. Their schedules didn't allow them to take another class and study hour didn't meet third hour. Aine hung her head in shame. Great, even being a banshee ruined the one thing she did well, sing. She ignored everyone as she bolted from the room heading for the counselor's office. She'd take anything else third hour, even another P.E. class. She got into Art.

She handed the art teacher her pass.

"Ah, another victim," The art teacher joked. "Can you draw?" Aine shook her head. "Paint?" Again, Aine shook her head.

"Well, you'll fit right in. Take a seat at the back table, we're making collages today. Grab a bunch of magazines, some scissors, glue and a poster board. I expect you to work quietly. Have at it." She pointed to the supplies. Aine took what she needed and headed to the empty back table. She sat down leafing through a magazine. *Great, just great.*

After third hour Aine walked to her locker. Grace's locker was next to hers. That used to be Sarah's locker. *I guess Sarah changed lockers.* Much to Aine's amazement Grace got her locker open on the first try.

"I can never get mine to work," Aine said. Chad came up to her slipping his arms around her waist pulling her close to him from behind. "Hi, Chad," she announced smiling at Grace.

"Hi yourself Aine, I missed you."

"Since first hour? Poor baby. Oh, this is Grace, she's a transfer student. Grace, this is Chad."

Grace smiled wider. "Nice to meet you Chad. What class do you have next, Aine?"

"Math 10 with Mr. Brady. My least favourite."

"Oh, great, me too. Can you show me the way? This school is so big even the map they gave me gets me lost!" She waited.

"Sure I'll walk with you. See you at lunch, Chad."

"Bad news, they switched my lunch hour, I'm heading to lunch now. My fourth hour teacher decided he wanted lunch before class not after."

"Oh? See you in English Lit then."

"I have that too," Grace piped up. "What hour?"

"Sixth," Aine and Chad said at the same time.

"Great," Grace gushed. "See you, Chad." As soon as Chad walked away she said, "He seems nice. Cute too."

"He is nice," Aine said. She began to get a strange feeling but it passed before she could name it.

"I'm sorry about Choir, it's just that your singing voice is so high it hurts. Maybe you could sing lower?"

"I already dropped it, I'm in Art now." She didn't want to talk about Choir.

When Aine walked into English Lit she saw Chad and Grace sitting together. Grace threw her head back laughing at something Chad had said. He spotted Aine in the doorway and smiled at her. She felt her

74

footsteps drag as she went to sit in the only other empty seat three rows over and two seats back from Chad. *Now I know how Sarah feels.* Aine played with her pen clicking and unclicking it until Mrs. Mahoney took it away from her with a smile. She handed it right back.

"Keep the clicking to a minimum, Aine." Aine nodded laying the pen on her desk. Grace scooted her desk right behind Chad's. She took the opportunity to tug at his shirt until he turned around then giggled. She did it several times. He didn't seem annoyed though, just amused. The bell finally rang. Aine jumped out of her seat. She took off out the door to her locker. She managed to get it open, throw her books in, and take the books out she'd need for the weekend. She saw Chad and Grace coming; he bent down to hear what she was saying. Grace looked up at him with an adoring look. *Oh, brother.* She waited until they were in earshot.

"Look, Chad I can't go out with you tonight, family emergency. I'll see you on Monday." She left before he could say anything. She heard him call her name but she pretended she didn't.

The first bus was full so she waited for
the second bus. She glanced back at the
arch. She saw Chad getting into his mother's
car and Grace getting in too. *Great.*
Wonderful. She dug in her bookbag for her
math book. Damn. It must be still in her
locker. She ran back inside to get it. The
lock refused to budge. She tried it several
times. It would not open. She had bad locker
ju-ju or bad locker karma or something. She
leaned against it tears stinging.

"Need something Ms. O'Shea?" Mr.
Collins, the science teacher.

"I can't get my locker open. The
combination lock won't work."

"If you give me your combination I can
try it." She gave it to him and it opened. She
mumbled thanks to him. He nodded. She got
the math book and slammed the locker shut.
It echoed briefly in the now-deserted
hallway. She got a creepy feeling. *I better*
go.

She walked as far as the end of the hall
when a sign caught her attention. POOL
with an arrow pointing. She followed the
sign to the pool. The synchronized swim
team was practicing. She sat on the
bleachers watching them. The warmth and

humidity in the pool area made her hair frizz. Even here, next to the pool she felt the calling of the sea. It was a steady ache inside of her but it got stronger if she was near the ocean. When someone in the Kavanaugh family, one of the original Irish families was sick or dying made the ache stronger. Those were the times she couldn't control the urge to wail and keen. She sighed. A girl walked through the bleachers and sat next to her.

"Hello," the girl said. She looked like a freshman.

"Hello," Aine said staring at the swimmers.

"You can see me?" the girl asked.

"Of course I can see you, you're sitting right next to me," Aine said shaking her head.

"I mean, most people can't see me. In fact you are the first one that has been able to see me since it happened."

Aine, lost in her thoughts barely heard her. "Since what happened?"

"Since I drowned here last summer." Aine's head whipped around to stare at the girl. She now appeared to be wet, her dark hair hanging around her face, dripping water off the ends.

"Drowned? As in, drowned? As in, died?"

The girl nodded. "This cute boy didn't like me and I thought he did. He asked my best friend out instead and told her he thought I was ugly and stupid." The girl watched the swimmers. "I wanted to join the swim team that's why I came here. I practiced every morning for weeks. But, they turned me down. Afterwards, I came here when no one was around and let the water take me." She sighed. "Now I can't leave here. I spend all my days and nights in the pool area watching the swimmers. I see my friends but none of them see me. I didn't know it would be so lonely to be dead." Aine thought the girl might be delusional. Aine put her hand on the girl's leg and it passed through to the bench below. Aine jumped up. The girl smiled up at her. Her hair was dry again.

"Don't be scared. You're the first person I've been able to talk to. Please stay. Tell me what I should do next. I don't know what to do." She began to cry. Aine tried to pat her shoulder but her hand went through her again. *I forgot.*

"What's your name?" Aine asked.

"Ellen Hayes. I'm fifteen. I'll always be fifteen." She stared at Aine. "Will you help me?"

"I'll try. Look I have to go home but let me think about this and I'll come back as soon as I can, I promise. Fennen will know what to do. He's a...well, he's a faerie."

"Aren't you a faerie too?" Ellen wanted to know.

"How did you know I was a...never mind. I'll find you after I talk to Fennen, okay?"

Ellen nodded. "Okay." She went back to watching the swimmers. Aine ran almost tripping on the bleachers. The only unlocked door connected the pool to the outside. She went out the door to the parking lot. She felt as if she was surrounded by people but no one was there. *What is happening to me?*

6

Fennen smiled at Aine when she walked in the door.

"You're late and your mom is upset about it. She thought Grianne got you."

"I forgot my math book in my locker. I had to go back for it and I missed the bus."

Her mom came out of the kitchen wiping her hands. Aine knew her mom felt stressed out when she either dug in the garden or baked. Today she baked. Powdered sugar on the end of her nose and on both cheeks signaled her stress level as being high.

"You're late," her mom said. Aine tried not to laugh but her mom did look ridiculous. "What is so funny?" her mom asked.

"You have sugar on your nose," Fennen pointed out. She ignored him.

"That doesn't change the fact that you are late Aine and we...I was worried!" Her mom sat down in the closest chair.

"I know, I'm sorry, mom. I got interested in watching the swim team practice." *And in talking to a dead girl.*

"Next time call, you know how dangerous dark faeries are."

80

"No, I don't. I mean you and Fennen have told me they are dangerous but how would I know otherwise? How do I know this isn't some elaborate ploy to get me to come right home after school?" Aine looked at Fennen. "Oh, and the double date is off. It seems like Chad is more interested in the new girl than in me." Aine went to her room shutting the door behind her.

A knock a few minutes later interrupted her. She put her book down.

"Come in."

"I brought you a couple of lemon bar cookies dusted with powdered sugar fresh out of the oven, her mom said. Aine noticed her mom's face had no traces of the powdered sugar any longer. "And tea." She set the plate of cookies down along with the cup. "Want to talk?"

Aine shook her head. "No, not right now. I want to finish this novel for English. Then I'm going to finish my weekend homework so I can have some time to relax tomorrow. Want to see a movie with me?"

"Oh, honey, I'd love to but I got called in to work."

"What exactly is your work, Mom? You never told me exactly only that you have an office."

"I work for the CIF. Just like Fennen. I keep track of the faeries in the Midwest Region. Sort of like a witness protection program but for faeries. If they get detected by humans I relocate them with new identities, names, documents and so on."

"So, you are a marshal like on TV?"

"Yes, only in the CIF they call us FG's."

"And that means?"

"Faerie guards. I joined the CIF right after we moved here. That's how I met Fennen and Patrick's mom."

"You met Patrick's mom before I did? Oh, right the whole marriage at birth thing."

"Yes, now I have to relocate a faerie in Chicago who's been too noticeable. He's a stand up comedian and we don't encourage our faeries to have jobs in show business. Too much media attention is bad for us."

"And what about you and me? Can't you relocate us so Grianne doesn't find us?"

"It wouldn't matter where we went ,Aine she'd find us. As soon as she makes a move we'll capture her. Fennen is well-trained in capturing dark faeries." Her mom smiled."Maybe we could do a movie on Sunday? I should have everything done by tomorrow night. I have to fly to Chicago to take the faerie to his new location."

"That's why you travel so much?"

"Yes."

"Do you, I mean do you have wings?" Aine couldn't remember ever seeing her mother without a covering of some sort on.

"No, I don't. Some of the faeries do but most of us look like ordinary humans. That's why we can blend in so well."

"What about other beings like werewolves, vampires, demons, aliens; are they real?

"No, there are no aliens Aine. That's from watching too many Sci Fi movies." Aine's eyes widened.

"But there are other beings? Her mom nodded. "Have you ever met a vampire?"

"Sure, they usually stay away from faeries; we are too bright for them."

"Bright?"

"We live in the light, they prefer the dark."

"Are there any vampires around here?"

"Most of them are in the big cities like LA and New York, New Orleans, London, Paris, Moscow, Bucharest, Berlin." She shrugged. "But I don't keep up with them so I'm not sure if any are here or not. Fennen might know."

"And if I met one how would I know?" Aine asked.

"You'd know. Every time we meet another being we get a feeling. Sort of like a tingling but not exactly."

"Do you see ghosts?" Aine asked thinking about Ellen.

"Ghosts? No, I don't see dead spirits but your Granny Kate could see them, talk to them and help them move on. It's part of being a banshee…oh." Her mom looked at her. Aine nodded.

"That's why I was late today. I met a girl at school. She turned out to be dead. She drowned in the pool two years ago."

"Did you get her name?" Fennen asked walking in. Aine jumped.

"Will you stop doing that?" she asked. "You startle me every time."

"Did she give you her name?" he asked again.

"Yes, her name is…was Ellen Hayes. She committed suicide by drowning herself in the pool at school."

"I'll check it out," he left.

"What does he need to check out?" Aine asked.

"He wants to make sure a girl did drown by that name and that it isn't Grianne pretending to be a dead girl to get close to you."

"It wasn't Grianne. I didn't get any funny feelings around her. I told her we'd help her. Can we? I mean, can I help her?"

"Yes. Fennen will show you what to do." She smiled taking a bite of one of the cookies. "These are good. If you finish before six I'll take you out to Chinese and then we can come home and watch a movie. Your choice."

"Really? My choice?"

"Yes, but nothing with horror or killing in it. Oh, and no romance. I'd prefer not to watch anything animated either."

"Something with vampires?" Aine teased.

"If it's not too gory or too graphic."

"I know just the one," Aine smiled.

Saturday morning dawned clear. Aine stretched before getting out of bed. She heard her mom making tea humming under her breath. She hummed an Irish lullaby that Granny Kate taught her. Aine hummed the same tune pulling on jeans and a tee shirt. She bounded into the kitchen giving her mom a hug around the waist.

"Morning Mom, can I have the car today? I can drop you off at your office."

" I'm heading to the airport and its all freeway driving. I called a shuttle service they should be here in a half hour."

"So, it's okay if I drive the car?"

"Sure, just make sure you fill up the tank and don't let Fennen drive, he'll drive on the wrong side of the road!"

"I won't, thanks. How long will you be gone?"

"Just today, I should be back by tonight or tomorrow morning at the latest." She handed Aine a cup of tea. "I have my cell if you need me. Fennen will be here too."

It was bad enough her mom would be gone for the day but Fennen followed her from room to room. She finally went into her bedroom and slammed the door to keep him out. She tried her mom's cell but it went straight to Voice Mail. She went on her laptop to check Facebook and saw that both Jess and Sarah had seen the latest movie last night and gave it a good review. She sighed. At one time they would've called her to go with them. She decided to get off Facebook when she saw a friend request from Grace. She accepted it even though she was convinced that Grace was after Chad. Not that she cared, Aine didn't really like him enough to be upset about him dating Grace. How sad is that? She jumped when her phone rang.

"Hello?"

"It's me cuz, how ya been?" Claire said in her lilting Irish brogue.

"Claire! It's great to hear from you. Patrick told me you are going to Harvard Law now."

"Yes, I am and he told me you broke up with him. Is that true?"

"I guess. I mean I feel like I'm too young to be engaged."

"That's cool. So you don't mind if we date?"

"You and me?" Aine joked.

"No, me and Patrick of course. He's so dreamy."

"Sure, go for it." But Aine felt her heart sink and she was nauseous. What did that mean?

"I'm glad you approve cuz. Well, we kinda slept together last night."

"Oh?" *I don't want to hear this.*

"You're not pissed are you?"

"No, we're broken up." Aine decided to change the subject. "What colour is your hair now?" Claire had a tendency to colour her hair on a whim. Claire laughed.

"Well, it used to be blonde with green tips but now it's blonde with a blue streak in the front and cut short."

"Send me a pix."

"Will do. Are you coming to Ireland this summer?"

"No, probably not." Aine wanted to tell Claire about the dark faerie but couldn't figure out how to get the words out.

"Well, see ya cuz. Tell your Ma I said hello." *You mean, the queen of the faeries?*

"Okay. 'Bye." Aine burst into tears as soon as she hung up the phone. She had no one in her life now. Patrick was gone. He was with Claire. In the back of her mind she thought that eventually they'd be together. They were supposed to be destined for each other, weren't they? She threw herself on her bed sobbing.

In the middle of the night she got the green silk banshee dress out that Granny Kate had given her. She had stashed it at the back of her closet. She felt an urge to put it on. She had forgotten how soft and light the dress was until she had it on again. It floated over her hips. She fingered the beading on the collar. The drooping ends of the sleeves reminded her of a medieval dress. Maybe she'd wear it to the Renaissance Faire this summer. If she could find someone to go with her. She used to go with Jess and Sarah. Every year since they were in elementary school. It was their tradition. *No*

longer.   Her feelings overwhelmed her and
she began to sing a low tone. It lightened her
heart a little so she sang again. She didn't
care if Fennen heard her or not, she needed
to sing. She sang another note, that note
turned into another one and a song emerged.
It was in Irish. She stood in the center of her
room singing a sad song. The ending of it
echoed throughout the house. Fennen came
in, he gathered her in his arms crooning
words in Irish to her.

"Shush, it'll be okay Aine. I'm here for
you, sh—it'll be fine." She stepped out of
the embrace staring at his face.

"What is it? What's happened? Is it my
mom?"

"The plane went down just outside of
Cork. No survivors. I wanted to wait until
morning to tell you but I forgot you'd figure
it out on your own."

"Cork? But, she went to Chicago, it's
not her," Aine insisted suddenly relived.

"She decided to take the faerie to live in
our world. The easiest way to get to there is
through the doorways in Ireland. There are
hundreds located all over the country. Here,
there are only a few. The closest one is

outside of L.A." Aine couldn't listen to him any longer. She ran down the hall.

"Mom? Mom? Where are you?" Aine ran to her mom's empty bedroom. She ran from room to room searching for her mom. She ran out into the yard yelling.

"Mom? Mom? I'm here, don't leave me alone Mom, please?" She fell to her knees sobbing out her sorrow. Her voice rose as she keened and wailed. She barely registered Fennen lifting her into his arms.

He carried her into the house depositing her on the sofa. She struggled to get back up still having a strong urge to keen. He pushed her back down and gently covered her with an afghan as he said some words over her. She stopped crying. The keening stopped too. A numb feeling washed over her. She clutched the edge of the afghan to her chin. Fennen sat down in the leather chair across from her. He watched her with an intense gaze. Aine pulled her eyes from him and stared at the front door instead. Any minute now her mom would walk through the door. She kept watching the door expecting it to open. She fell asleep waiting.

7

It was as if a door to Faerieland suddenly opened. The house was full of faeries. Aine woke up to voices whispering phrases all around her, "the queen is missing", "what will happen now?", "who did this?" and various other comments Aine did not want to hear. The most disturbing comment of all was said by Fennen.

"I guess this means you are the Queen of the Faeries now, Aine. I mean, Your Majesty." Aine nearly lost it but held it in.

"What do you mean?" she asked through a clenched jaw. She saw faeries hovering in the background. There were so many! Some of them had wings, all of them were the size of humans. The ones with wings fluttered near the windows occasionally looking out. Aine wasn't sure if they kept watch or just wanted to be outdoors. They all spoke the same language, Gaelic or as they called it in Ireland, Irish. Aine could understand Irish.

"Be quiet!" Fennen yelled. The room quieted. "The Queen is about to speak."

"First of all, I am not the Queen, my mother is. She is not dead, she is just missing," Aine said. She heard audible sighs travel around the room.

"The dark faeries have her," piped up a young faerie with bright yellow wings fluttering near the doorway. All eyes stared at her.

"How do you know, Dilly?" Fennen asked.

She shrugged. "I feel it. I agree with the princess, the Queen is not dead." The murmuring started again. Fennen yelled again.

"Let the acting Queen speak," he yelled. All of their eyes moved to her. The faeries waited for her to speak.

She cleared her throat, her thoughts raced around. What could she say to appease these faeries? She wasn't their queen she was only the daughter of a queen, how odd was that? Fennen looked at her. She cleared her throat again. What do you call faeries?

"Fellow faeries---," she began. "I believe my mother, your queen, is not dead. She is missing, perhaps kidnapped. You need to go back to your daily lives and to act as if she is not missing." Loud mutterings assaulted her ears. She held up her hands for silence. They quieted down.

"No, listen to me, if she has been taken by the dark faeries then we will know soon enough." Aine took a deep breath, "And if she died in that plane crash, we will know that too."

"The Queen will count on us to rescue her," one of the faeries said.

"We cannot abandon her to the dark faeries," said another.

"And if she has died we need to give her a proper faerie burial and appoint a new Queen," said yet another. Fennen held up his hands and the room quieted once more.

"We can speculate but until we know what happened to Queen Fiona, we can do nothing except wait." He looked at Aine. "The Princess is right; we should go about our daily lives as if nothing has happened. The CIF will search for the Queen. As soon as we know what has happened to the Queen, we will summon you." He looked at the crowd. They muttered but began to disperse. Fennen pointed to Dilly."Dilly, please stay." He smiled at Aine. "Dilly is the Queen's most trusted advisors. She should stay with us until we know more."

She nodded. This was surreal. Last year she was a high school student, then she found out she was a banshee and now not only is she a banshee but she is a Princess and her mother is the Queen of the Faeries. Fennen came over to her.

"I'll make us some tea, shall I?" Aine nodded. *Where is Mom?*

Aine went to school even though she would have preferred to go with Fennen. He planned to take the next flight to Chicago to see if he could pick up Fiona's trail. The faerie she was relocating was also missing. Fennen made Aine go to school.

"You should go to maintain a sense of normalcy. I want you to take the car there and back. Do not ride the bus." He smiled at her. "I don't know when I'll be back but Dilly is here to protect you." He motioned to Dilly. "Can you go to school with Aine?"

"Sure, I'd love to." Aine shook her head at the two of them.

"No, there is no way I can explain another Irish cousin, this one with wings!"

Dilly laughed. "I can make myself invisible or nearly invisible using faerie glamour. No one will see me except you and Grianne, if she is there."

"Fine, but don't get in my way," Aine grumbled. It felt odd to drive the car without her mom in the passenger seat but Dilly kept up a running conversation with her in order to distract her. Aine went straight to the office to get a parking sticker so her car wouldn't get towed. She put the sticker on the inside of the windshield and headed to class. Futtering her wings as she flew to keep up with Aine Dilly got jostled this way and that and finally gave up trying to fly and walked next to Aine. Dodging elbows and backpacks Dilly tried to keep up.

"Is it always so crowded?" she complained. They were at Aine's locker. Aine tried the lock sure it wouldn't open but to her amazement, it did. She dug out her books stuffing her backpack inside and headed to her first class. Dilly ran alongside her. Aine bumped into Chad going through the door at the same time he went through.

"Hey, watch it, oh, it's you. Hi, Aine. How are you?" he smiled at her but it was a cautious smile.

"I'm okay I guess." She wondered if she should tell him about her mom. She decided

not to as soon as Dilly put her arm on hers.
Dilly took a seat on the floor next to Aine's
desk. Aine ignored her as she did her work.

After school Aine took Dilly to the pool.
"There is Ellen. She's over there." Ellen sat
on the bleachers watching the water in the
pool. No swim team practiced today so the
water was still. A strong odor of chlorine
hung in the air. Aine waved to Ellen who
waved back at her.

She introduced Dilly to Ellen. "Ellen?
This is Dilly, she's a faerie too."

"I can tell by the wings," Ellen said
looking at Aine.

"Right. Well, anyway. I wanted to ask
you something. My mom is missing. Her
plane went down on Saturday in Ireland and
I figured that if anyone would know if she
were dead, it would be you. So, is she?
Dead, I mean?" Aine waited unaware she
held her breath.

"I don't know if she is or not," Ellen said.
"But, I can't see any new spirits around you
so probably not."

Aine let out her breath. "I knew that if
anyone could figure it out it would be you."
She turned to Dilly. "Now that she know

she's not dead we can concentrate on finding her."

"Hey, O'Shea, who you talking too? The voices in your head? 'Cuz none of us can't see anyone standing there!" Courtney Briggs. The most popular girl in school. She was head cheerleader with a perfect body, had a 4.00 Grade Point Average, volunteered at the children's hospital on a weekly basis, sang in a clear high soprano, acted in the school plays, danced in the local dance company, played flute and piano flawlessly and was rumored to have slept with the entire football team and the track team. Aine doubted that was true but still…oh and she hated Aine. On sight. Aine wasn't sure why but she took every opportunity she had to ridicule and humiliate her. And this was the perfect opportunity. Her posse was with her. Four Courtney look-a-likes, also cheerleaders but not as talented as Courtney. Or as smart. Nicky, Jackie and Mandy or as Aine liked to call them, Larry, Curly and Moe, the three Stooges.

Dilly frowned at the girls now walking toward them. "Who are they? What do they want?"

"Shush," Aine said but Courtney heard her.

"Asking the voices to be quiet again?" she smirked.

"What do you want Courtney?"

"I just wanted to tell you that you left these in Chad's locker and he said to tell you he doesn't want them." She dangled a black thong in front of Aine's face.

"Not mine. They look more like your style," Aine said.

"That's not what Chad said. He said he got into your pants at the dance and now he can't get rid of you."

She had to be talking about Sarah. God, Courtney was an idiot. "I didn't go to the dance with Chad."

Courtney looked at her posse; her beautiful face looked puzzled for an instant then cleared as if too much emotion would make it wrinkle. Aine did not think that would happen because of all the Botox in Courtney's face but miracles still came true, didn't they?

"I thought you said she went to the dance with Chad," Courtney said to Mandy who shrugged, a bored look on her face.

"It was one of them, I can't remember all their names," she whined. "Maybe it was one of the other two."

I snatched the thong out of Courtney's hands. "Give it to me, it is mine after all." I stuffed them in my pocket. "Now, leave me alone!"

She smirked at me again. "I knew it. You are a freak. Who sleeps with a boy on their first date? Freaks and losers like you, that's who. Let's go girls." She snapped her fingers at the girls. The three of them turned and sashayed out of the pool area laughing uproariously.

"Is it yours?" Dilly asked. Aine shook her head.

"No, they belong to a friend of mine---a former friend---and I didn't want her to find out that Courtney had them. Of course it'll be all over the Internet by tonight."

And it was. Courtney put up the picture of the throng on her Facebook page with the caption: What Freak Left These in Chad's Car on Prom Night? Yes, our one and only Freaky girl. A picture of Aine sitting alone at lunch with a book covering most of her face accompanied the caption. Various

comments ranged from "Freak!" to "OMG
she is so weird" to "Chad? How could you?"
Aine shut her laptop with a groan. Fennen
stood behind her making her jump.

"Fennen, I asked you to stop doing that."

"Who's thong was that?" he wanted to
know.

"None of your business. What are you
doing to find my mom?" She glared at him.
"I thought you flew to Chicago to pick up
my mom's trail."

"The CIF is working on it." Dilly chose
that moment to fly in and settle on the sofa.

"Do you have school tomorrow?" she
asked Aine who nodded.

"Yes, I have school every day, why?"

"Every day?" Dilly moaned. "I don't
think I can go again. It was too crowded for
me." She held out a wing to them. "See? It's
bruised." Aine peered at the spot. It didn't
look any different to her.

"We did find out that Mom isn't dead,"
Aine said to Fennen. His eyes widened.

"And you didn't think it was important to
tell me that until now? How do you know
she's not dead?"

"The ghost girl told me. Ellen. She said
there were no new spirits around me."

Fennen rubbed his hands together. "This is good news. I will inform the CIF. Now we know that the Queen has been kidnapped by Grianne." Dilly smiled but stopped when she realized Aine glared at her.

"I'm sorry, I'm glad Queen Fiona is alive. Although Grianne will probably torture her before killing her. She'll die a painful death."

"Dilly!" Fennen said with a sharp tone. She winced and went back to rubbing her bruised wing.

Aine went to her room to finish her homework. She thought about what Dilly said. What if her mom is being tortured? What if Grianne kills her? Aine picked up her cell phone. She fingered it trying to decide. She gave in and pressed Patrick's number. He answered on the first ring.

"Aine? What's wrong?" She sighed. Dating a faerie was different than dating a human. Faerie's always knew when something was wrong.

"My mom has been kidnapped by a dark faerie named Grianne."

"When?"

"Saturday night I guess or Sunday morning," Aine said.

"Where's Fennen? Why didn't he call me?" Patrick wanted to know.

"He's here keeping an eye on me along with Dilly, one of mom's agents."

"Do you want me to come to you?" he asked. His voice spoke volumes. He still loved her!

"Yes, I mean, no. I mean, is Claire okay with you flying here?"

"Claire and I aren't dating Aine. I know she told you we were but we aren't."

"I…did you sleep with her?" Aine hated herself for asking.

"Yes, one night. I'm sorry. It won't happen again. I had too much to drink." He hesitated. "I still want to marry you, Aine. I love you."

"I know. I have to find my mother Patrick. I can't think about anything else right now."She tried to get the image of Claire and Patrick together out of her head.

"I understand. I'll catch the Red Eye. Expect me sometime tonight. Oh, and tell Fennen he's in trouble for not calling me!"

Aine finished her homework. She jumped when she saw a shadowy figure on her bed. Dilly took off her glamour with a smile.

"I'm sorry if I startled you, Aine. How are you?"

"I'm fine, Dilly. What do you want?"

"Just to tell you that there is a visitor here to see you. Fennen wanted me to let you know she's waiting out there." She pointed to the door.

"When he asks you to tell me something it's generally acceptable to knock on a person's door, wait for them to tell you it's okay to come in, then go in and give them a message." Geez, were these faeries not around humans at all?

"Okay, Aine. Should I tell her you want her to come in?"

"Who is it?"

"Her name is Sarah." Sarah, here? What could she possibly want? Aine left Dilly on the bed to go in search of Sarah. Fennen entertained her in the kitchen with his Irish jokes. None of them were funny. Sarah smiled slightly at him. What's not to smile at? A cute Irish guy giving you all his attention would be Sarah's idea of heaven on earth.

"Hey, Sarah," Aine said. Sarah jumped off the stool to embrace Aine.

"Oh, Aine, I am so sorry. I..er.." She
looked at Fennen. He didn't get the hint.

"Go find Dilly or something," Aine
commanded. He bowed leaving them alone.

"Wow, that was different," Sarah said
sitting back on the stool. Aine sat too.
"Look Aine I wanted to say---"

"You don't have to say anything Sarah, I
understand."

"No, you don't. Just listen for a minute
will you?"

"Sure, go ahead."

"I saw Courtney's website. I saw the
thong. They were mine. You knew they
were mine but you said they were yours."
Tears shone in Sarah's eyes. "Thank you for
that."

Aine pulled the thong out of her pocket
and held them up. "I believe these are
yours," she said. The two of them laughed
hugging again.

"I can't believe I slept with that creep,"
Sarah said stuffing the thong in her bag.

"I can't believe I planned to go out on a
date with him," Aine said.

Sarah smiled again. "I am sorry I treated
you like you were a freak, Aine. I want to be
friends again, if you want to."

"Of course I do." Aine hesitated. "What about Jess? Does she still hate me too?"

"No, I told her what you did for me and she forgave you too."

"Wait a minute, forgave me? For what? I didn't do anything, you guys thought I did!" Aine shook her head.

"I know, we are sorry, Aine." Sarah hung her head for a moment. She looked up. "I heard about your mom.. Jess wanted to be here too but she had to babysit again."

"My mom is missing. I think she's been kidnapped."

Sarah's eyes widened. "Kidnapped? Who would kidnap your mom? She's a real estate agent isn't she?"

"No, she's the Queen of the Faeries and a dark faerie named Grianne is behind it. She plans on getting my mom's crown so she can be Queen of all the Faeries. Oh, and BTW I am Princess Aine. But, you can call me, Your Royal Highness." Sarah guffawed almost falling off the stool. Aine laughed until she cried. She ended up sobbing on Sarah's shoulder.

Sarah rubbed her back soothing her as she kept saying over and over, "Shush, it'll be all right, Aine, shush. We'll find her, shush."

8

Patrick arrived in the middle of the night. She heard his voice as he talked to Fennen. Her door opened but she pretended to be asleep. She'd deal with him in the morning.

He closed the door softly. The low rumble of their voices lulled her back to sleep.

Fennen handed her a cup of tea as soon as she showed up in the kitchen. She took a drink looking around for Patrick. Where's Patrick? Almost as if he heard her thoughts he appeared. He rushed over to hug her. She hugged him back but it was brief. Fennen watched them.

"Hi, Patrick," she said sitting down at the breakfast counter.

"Hi, yourself. You look tired." She nodded.

Fennen put a bagel down in front of her. She took a bite.

"Where are you staying?" she asked.

107

"Here," he said. "Dilly and Fennen are still here. We feel like you are in grave danger, Aine." She shrugged. What's new? She took another bite of her bagel before standing up.

"Look, I have to get ready for school. We can catch up later."

His eyebrows went up. "School? I thought you'd stay home since the Queen is missing."

"No, I told her she should go," Fennen said. "Maintain her normal routine, not draw attention to herself."

"Oh," Patrick looked at Fennen then back at Aine. "Well, I guess that's a good idea. Want me to come to school with you?"

"No, Dilly is my school faerie," Aine joked. She looked at the clock on the wall. "I better finish getting ready. I'll see the two of you after school." She took off before either one could say anything. She felt the tension in the room between Patrick and Fennen and it made her nervous.

At least school would be tolerable now that Sarah and Jess were back in her life. Aine felt her steps lighten as she approached her locker. She spotted Grace and waved.

"Hey, Grace, where ya been?"

"Sick. Puked my guts out for a couple of days. I'm better now. What's happening with you?" She watched Aine get her books out of her locker. For some reason the lock didn't stick any more.

"My mom is officially missing."

"Yeah?" The two of them fell in step as they headed to their first class.

"Her plane went down and they can't find her." A dark faerie has her. *Yeah, like I'd tell anyone that.*

"You think she's dead?" Grace asked standing near the doorway of Aine's classroom.

"No, I don't. I think she'll turn up."

"You never know, do you?" Grace said turning to go. Aine got the feeling again. That weird tingly feeling. She dismissed it as too much caffeine or not enough before heading to her seat.

Aine went to the pool area looking for Ellen again. She saw her lurking in the corner watching someone with a frown on her face. Aine looked closer and saw that Ellen stared at Grace who stared back at her.

It seemed like Ellen didn't want Grace there.
Is she afraid of her.? Aine raised her hand in
a wave to Ellen.

"Ellen?" she called. Ellen looked at her,
nodded and vanished. Grace turned and
smiled. She wandered over to Aine.

"Hey, Aine, what are you doing here?"

"Who were you talking to?" Aine asked.

"No one, I was just thinking. This place
is great for that since it's so quiet if no one
is practicing."

"I thought I saw you looking at
someone," Aine said. Did Grace see Ellen
too? And if she did, what does that mean?

"I saw someone too, over there in the
corner," Aine pointed to where Ellen had
been standing. Grace followed her finger
staring at the wall. She shook her head.

"Nope, I didn't see anyone. What did
you see?"

"Nothing, I guess. No one." Aine
wondered why Grace wouldn't admit she
saw Ellen. And how could she see a dead
girl if she wasn't a faerie?

Grace walked over to the bleachers and
sat down. Aine followed her. The two of
them sat without speaking for a moment.

"My mom is still missing," Aine said.

"You should go look for her," Grace said staring at the pool.

"Her plane went down in Ireland, I can't." Could she?

The airline called. The families of the missing or dead are invited to a memorial on the coast near where the plane went down. The airline would fly Aine there and back free of charge. The memorial will be held in three days. Aine wanted to go. She hung up smiling. She didn't tell Fennen. Or Patrick. Or Dilly.

On the morning of the memorial she packed her backpack. A cab would pick her up to take her to the airport. She left the house shutting the door behind her. The sunrise turned the morning sky to a pinkish hue; there was an eerie feel to the air. A light mist lay over the ground. Aine shivered as she waited for the taxi to arrive. Someone walked toward her. Aine thought she should go back inside but didn't want to wake the household. She stood her ground. As the person approached she realized it was Grace.

"Grace? What are you doing here?"Aine asked.

"I heard about the memorial. I thought you might want company. I have my own ticket." She waved a piece of paper in the air smiling. How odd. But before Aine could think about it the taxi pulled up to the curb. She didn't want the driver to honk the horn so she rushed toward it. Grace hung back with a smile on her face.

"Well, come on, get in. I guess we're going to Ireland together,"Aine said scooting over so Grace could get in next to her. Grace smiled slamming the door. The front door to the house opened and Fennen stood there in a tee shirt and shorts. His hair stood on end. He must've heard the door shut. Aine waved to him from the rear window. He called to her but she ignored him. Grace watched her wave.

"Who's that? Your boyfriend?"

"No, he's my bro..he's a friend." Aine settled into the seat for the 45 minute ride to the airport. Grace pulled out her iPod, plugged in ear phones and settled back too. Aine fell asleep as soon as they hit the freeway.

Aine's airline pass allowed her and Grace to bypass most of the lines. They waited to go through the security check. Finally, they were allowed to board Aer Lingus.

"Have you flown before?" Aine asked Grace. They searched for their seats. Aine hoped for a window seat.

"Yes, many times, you?" Grace asked. Grace found their seats and sat down closest to the window. She held her backpack on her lap. Aine pointed to it.

"You can't hold that, you have to put it in storage during the flight." The flight attendant came through helping them put their bags in the overhead storage. Aine sat down with a sigh.

"I've flown a couple of times. To Ireland and back. I visited my Great-Grandmother who died last Christmas."

"Oh? Sorry to hear that," Grace said. She waved to the flight attendant. "Can we get breakfast?"

"As soon as the plane is in the air I'll bring you a menu," the flight attendant said smiling. He had a lovely Irish accent.

"Thanks," Grace said. She turned to Aine. "I'm starving." Aine's phone began to ring. She looked at the display and grimaced.

"Who is it?" Grace asked.

"Someone I don't want to talk to," Aine said ignoring the phone. She put it on vibrate and stuck it in her pocket.

"No cell phones during the flight," the flight attendant said. Aine looked around. She didn't remember the airplane being this spacious before. "Are we in First Class?" Aine asked.

"Yes, your tickets were for First Class," he said moving on.

"How did you get a First Class ticket to Ireland?" Aine asked Grace.

She shrugged. "I wanted one next to you. I told them I was your sister."

"Oh, well, welcome to the family," Aine laughed. She opened the memorial brochure the airline had sent her. "It says we can stay in a hotel with the other families if we want. The actual memorial is on Sunday morning at 10am Ireland time. The return flight leaves Monday morning."

"I guess we miss a couple of days of school," Grace said. She had a window seat. She looked out the window. Aine craned her neck to see. Their seats were in the front of the plane. Aine shut her eyes as the plane took off. Once they were in the air the atmosphere around them seemed less tense. The flight attendant brought them a menu. Aine ordered fresh fruit and a bagel. Grace ordered the bacon and eggs, sausage and a biscuit with gravy. She was so thin Aine expressed surprise at how much she ordered.

"You like to eat a lot at breakfast?" Aine asked picking at her fruit plate.

"Yes, I guess I do. I'm always ravenous," Grace laughed taking a bite of her bacon.

The flight attendant brought them coffee. Aine sipped hers. She watched Grace eat. She was grateful Grace was with her. She knew she'd probably cry at the memorial and with Grace next to her she might not cry so much. She felt her phone vibrate in her pocket. She pulled it out. Voice Mails, three of them. She would listen to them once they landed. She smiled at Grace. They both slept after breakfast.

The flight landed on time. Last time Aine came to Ireland she flew to Dublin. This time she flew into Cork. She wanted to be close to her cottage on the Irish coast that

Ginny Ma left her. She planned on going there to see what shape the cottage was in and to show it to Grace.

Once they were on the ground her phone vibrated in her pocket. She ignored it. A man held up a sign and people gathered near him. Aine pointed to the sign.

"I think it's for us, come on," she said. The two of them walked over to the man. "Is this for the memorial?" Aine asked.

"Yes, I expect several family members. My name is Ian and I am the airline's official representative." He looked at a clipboard he held. "And your name is?"

"Aine O'Shea and this is Grace, my...er..."

"Sister," Grace said. "I'm her sister."

"Fine, the limo outside will take you to the hotel. Meals will be scheduled. The memorial is Sunday morning at 10 just down the coast. The limo's will take the family members there." He smiled at them but mostly at Grace who seemed to be flirting with him. "Any questions?"

"No, thanks, come on Grace." Aine led the two of them to the black limo outside. It stretched along the curb. Aine got in, Grace followed. Other people were already inside.

It looked like it could hold twenty people.
Aine sat in silence. So did Grace. Finally,
they had enough people so the driver took
off. He dropped them at the hotel. Aine and
Grace stood in line waiting to be checked in.
They got a room on the fourth floor. They
were handed a schedule of local activities,
meals in the dining room and a schedule of
the memorial activities. Flower wreaths
were available to purchase from a local
flower shop.

Aine put the schedule down and turned
to Grace with tears in her eyes.

"I can't handle all this right now, Grace.
I know I wanted to come but, my mom is
not dead. I feel it."

"What do you want to do?" Grace asked
laying across the bed staring at Aine.

"I guess I should call Patrick and Fennen
and tell them where I am. Then I want to eat
something. Let's go to the cottage I am
anxious to see it again."

"Okay, I'm game for whatever," Grace
said. "First on my list is a shower." She
headed into the bathroom. Aine sighed
punching in the number for her house.
Fennen answered on the first ring.

"Where are you?" he asked.

"I decided to go to the memorial for the families of the surviving members of the place crash."

"Your mother is not dead, she has been kidnapped by Grianne, you know this," Fennen said.

"I felt like I had to come to Ireland, don't ask me to explain, Fennen because I can't."

"Are you alone?" he asked.

She smiled into the phone. "No, one of my friends came with me. I'll be back on Monday morning, Fennen. This is something I have to do."

"Patrick wants to talk to you," he said in reply. Patrick came on the line.

"Be careful, Aine. I sense danger around you."

"I will be careful, I promise. Don't worry about me, Patrick, please?"

"I will fly to Cork and will be there tomorrow. Wait for me until you go to the cottage."

"How did you know I was…never mind." She forgot the faerie part of Patrick sensed things. She tried to send her senses outward but felt nothing. She shrugged. "I guess I'll see you tomorrow, Patrick," she said hanging up. Grace came out of the bathroom wrapped in a bathrobe with a towel around her head. She grinned at Aine.

"That felt good, are you next?"

"No, I'm okay." She still held the phone in her hand. Grace pointed to it.

"How are things at home with your boyfriend?"

"Fine, he's flying here tomorrow."

"What? Why?" Grace seemed overly concerned.

"I guess he doesn't trust me here alone," Aine said with a smile. Grace frowned.

"We better go to the cottage before he gets here."

"He wants me to wait," Aine said.

"But, you promised we could go today," Grace said pouting.

"Sure, we can go today. I can show you the Lough Gur where the Irish Goddess Aine lived," Aine smiled.

"Sounds like fun," Grace said going into the adjoining room to get dressed. She came out a few minutes later. "Let's go eat and then we can take a taxi to the cottage. I'm anxious to see the Lough Gur too. I read all about it on the Internet. Wasn't she supposed to come alive every seven years or something?"

"I think so, and if anyone drinks the water from the lake, they are poisoned but if they are a faerie, they live."

"Cool," Grace said. The two of them went to the dining room and identified themselves as guests of the airline by showing passes they were given. They ate then went outside to hail a taxi.

9

The trip to the cottage took almost half an hour, Aine sighed thinking about the cost.

"We should've taken a bus to Owen then a taxi from there."

"I'll pay for it, I'm the one that wanted to come to the cottage," Grace said pulling out her credit card.

"Are you sure?" Aine asked. "I can pay half if you want."

"Sure."

They got off in front of the cottage. It looked the same to Aine. She looked up at the chimney expecting to see smoke coming out of it and Ginny Ma to open the door for them. She sighed aloud.

"Come on in," she said to Grace. The two of them went inside. It smelled musty and damp. Aine went to the kitchen and ran the water for tea. Grace wandered around by herself. Aine went to the parlour and started a fire to warm the place up.

"It's chilly here," Grace said shivering.

"The fire will warm up the place soon," Aine said poking the wood so the flames would catch.

"This is cozy though, you own this?"

"Yes, I'm planning on living in it as soon as I'm done with high school." *And so is Patrick,* she thought but didn't say.

"It needs to have a major overhaul to bring it to the 21st century. Is there Internet access?"

Aine laughed. "There is barely electricity. When the wind blows or there's a storm, the electricity and the phone goes out."

"I need access to the Internet," Grace said pulling out her phone. "I can't even get a signal."

"You will be able to once we get back to Cork. Even Owel has an Internet café if you want to go there."

"Let's go see that lake you talked about."

"After we have tea," Aine said pouring both of them a cup.

"You've turned into a real Irish person," Grace said sipping hers. A wailing noise made Grace start. She almost dropped her cup. "What is that?" she asked.

"The seals out on the point. They live here year 'round. Want to see them?"

"Sure, first the seals, then the poison lake."

"Okay," Aine laughed. "Maybe we should stay at the cottage instead of at the hotel." Aine felt at home in the cottage. She felt like she belonged there.

Grace shook her head. "No Internet, remember?"

"Okay, we'll spend time with the seals, I'll show you the lake and then we can take a taxi back to Owel and a bus back to Cork."

"I'm ready," Grace said.

The two of them walked to the cliff and climbed down the wooden planks set in the hill. Aine reached the bottom first. She ran toward the water calling to the seals. Several of them appeared answering her call. She took off her shoes and socks and waded into the water. She longed to swim with the seals again. She raised her voice in song and the seals harmonized with her.

Grace hung back by the stairs. As she came forward the seals stopped singing and vanished under the water. Aine called to them again but they did not reappear.

"That's odd," Aine said. "They usually come when I call them."

"Maybe they're afraid of me," Grace said.

"Maybe." Grace took off her shoes and socks too and waded into the water with Aine.

"It's cold," Grace complained.

"It's the Irish Sea," Aine laughed. "I love it." She splashed Grace and Grace splashed her back.

"I'm going back, my feet are completely numb from the cold," Grace said walking back to the beach. She brushed off her feet before putting her socks and shoes back on. "Come on, Aine, let's find that poisoned lake."

"I'm coming," Aine felt reluctant to leave the water. She sensed the seals were nearby but for some reason they didn't want to show themselves.

She walked back to the beach and sat down next to Grace. She put her shoes and socks on again. She saw the seals far out in the water, their heads bopping in and out of the waves. She laughed at their antics. Grace frowned clearly not amused.

"Ready?" she asked standing up.

"Ready," Aine said. But, something held her back. She felt as if she should stay here with the seals and not go to the Lough Gur. Grace kept telling her to "hurry up" as Aine's steps faltered. The walk to the Lough Gur took them a while. Finally, the lake stood in front of them. During the summer months, like now, the lake filled with water. Signs on the beach warned swimmers against swimming due to the danger of contamination. Aine remembered that when she saw the lake it was winter and only a small bit of water was in the center of it.

"Where does this Irish Goddess live again?" Grace asked looking out at the water.

"In the center of the lake but, you can't get to it now, it's filled with water. I was able to get to the center in the winter when the water goes down. I tasted the water and it was sweet, not poisoned." Aine waited for Grace to comment on the fact that only faeries could drink from the Lough Gur and not get poisoned but she seemed oblivious to Aine's words. She continued to stare out at the water.

"Let's swim in it," Grace said beginning to peel off her clothes.

Aine, horrified, held up her hands. "No, Grace, see those signs? It's says the lake is too dangerous to swim in. The water is poisoned. If you get it in your mouth you'll get sick. Maybe you'll die. Please, don't do this." But Grace had taken off her clothes and stood in her bra and underwear before Aine.

"I'm going in. You coming?"

"No, Grace, stop!" Aine reached for her but Grace was too quick. She danced away from Aine and ran toward the water yelling something in a strange language. She jumped into the water making a huge splash. Aine felt like she had no choice but to follow her. She took off her clothes and dived into the water. It was warmer than the sea water. It felt like bath water. Aine swam up to where Grace swam. Grace flipped on her back floating on the water.

"See? It's fine Aine. Let's go further out. I want to see where the Irish Goddess lives." Grace swam away from Aine. *She swims like a seal.* Aine kept up with Grace but she felt a pull toward the shore like she should get out of the water. She followed Grace who floated in the center of the lake. She said some words aloud, words in a strange

126

language. The lake water began to bubble and surge. Suddenly, the water parted and dry land appeared beneath their feet.

Grace leaped onto the surface and spun around three times. She was now clothed in a dark green gown that swirled around her feet. Her hair was loose about her head and she had a circlet of gold around her forehead. Golden strands were weaved through her hair. Aine stood in a daze on the hard ground with the lake all around them. Grace laughed and scooped up some water with her hand. She swallowed it with a smile on her lips.

"It is sweet, Aine, you are right about that."

"Who are you?" Aine asked.

"You haven't guessed yet?" Grace asked. "You aren't as smart as I thought you were. I'm Grianne, of course. And I have your mother, and now, I have you." She clapped her hands and a doorway appeared.

"Welcome to the land of the Faeriedae. My land, where I am Queen." She grabbed Aine's hand and half-dragged her through the doorway. As soon as they went through the doorway it closed and Aine heard water

127

rushing. The lake filled itself in again behind the door.

"You have my mother?" Aine asked.

"I told you I did, she is safe for now. I want her to give her crown to me and if she does I will be Queen of all the Faeries. If she does not, well, let's just say she will regret it." Grace snapped her fingers and faeries arrived greeting her with bows and trays of food. She waved them away. "Bring me to Fiona, I have someone who wants to see her," Grianne said grinning at Aine. Small dark faeries surrounded her, herding her forward. She had no choice but to walk down the path that lay in front of her. They appeared to be in a dark forest under the lake. But, when she looked up she saw sky, not water. *How odd.*

"Where are we exactly?" Aine asked. Fear spread through her veins as she stared at the person she used to know as Grace. She looked much more imposing as Grianne than she ever had as Grace.

"We are in Faeriedae, I told you. It is the land of the faeries. There are many doorways to it but this one is my favourite. I love parting the waves and seeing the look on my prisoners faces," she laughed. She took a piece of a dark purple fruit from a tray one of the dark faeries held out to her and munched on it as they walked through the thick trees. Leaves under their feet crunched. She offered Aine a bite of the dark fruit but Aine shook her head. What will happen to her? Will she be able to escape? She wished she had listened to Patrick and waited for him to come before going to the cottage. She left her backpack at the hotel. She felt in her pocket for her iPhone. She had it but doubt she'd get a signal down here.

"Yeah, iPhones don't work in Faeriedae," Grianne commented. She stopped. They had come to a thicket of trees with branches interlaced over the path they had been following. Grianne said some words and they opened to reveal another path. She stepped through the branches and so did Aine. Her eyes widened. She saw a clearing filled with faeries coming and going. A city of sorts, she guessed. Grianne snapped her fingers again and a cart rolled up pulled by a large lizard creature.

"Get in," Grianne said as she settled down on a seat. "We still have a ways to go to my palace. Might as well be comfortable." Aine hesitated but a faerie behind her poked her in the back with something sharp so she got in and sat beside Grianne. The cart rumbled along the path. Grianne smiled as they made their way through the trees. Finally, they came to a golden palace glittering in the sunlight. Aine gasped.

"Beautiful," she muttered.

Grianne laughed. "Glad you approve, Aine. Now come on, I'm sure you are anxious to see your mother again."

As they walked up to the palace doors, the great wooden doors fashioned with golden doorknockers in the shape of goblins opened. Several faeries stood in a line bowing as the cart rolled in. Grianne jumped down with the help of a faerie. She held out a hand to Aine helping her down.

"I don't understand," Aine said. "I thought you were my friend."

Grianne laughed. "I know you did. That's why I became Grace. You needed a friend, so I became one. I thought it would be the only way to get close to you." She regarded Aine. "You are easy to fool, Aine. Don't you use your faerie senses at all?"

Aine remembered the strange tingly feeling she got whenever Grace was around her. She had ignored it.

"I guess not," she said hanging her head. How would she get them out of this? Maybe Patrick would help her. Somehow.

Grianne led them to a room, she flung open the door. There, on a small cot, lay her mother. Aine ran to her dropping onto her knees to embrace her.

"Mom! You're okay! Mom!" Her mother rose up to look at her. She did not look well. She looked pale and tired. Her clothes were in tatters and there were bruises on her cheek. "What happened to you, Mom?" She cradled her mother's head in her arms. She turned to Grianne who still stood at the door.

"If you hurt her in any way, I will hurt you," Aine said. She turned back to her mother and began to stroke her mother's hair. Her mother lay her head back down with a little smile on her lips.

"Tell your mother that if she gives up her crown to me then she can go free. You too. I'll let the two of you chat. I'll be back later for your answer." She slammed and locked the door behind her.

"Can you sit up, Mom?" Her mom nodded. She sat up gingerly. Aine sat next to her.

"I never wanted any of this to happen, Aine," her mom whispered.

"Can you tell me what happened?"

"I was in Chicago, looking to book a flight to Ireland for the faerie we were relocating. I was at the airport heading back from the ticket booth thinking about calling you when all of a sudden I felt a whoosh by my head and I was captured by two of Grianne's dark faeries. They brought me here." She sighed. "I let my faerie enchantments lapse. I go too complacent."

"It's been days since you were declared missing. The airplane you were supposed to be on went down near Cork. The airline is having a memorial for the surviving family members, that's why I'm here." She sighed. "Grace, I mean, Grianne pretended to be my friend and came with me for support. I felt I needed to be at the cottage again and near the seals. I don't know how she could've fooled me like that."

"She is a strong faerie. She used faerie glamour on you to disguise herself as your friend. I am sorry you had to come here too.

I hoped that Fennen could protect you." Her mom rubbed her cheek.

"Did they beat you, Mom?"

"Grianne did not like my answers to her questions so she had one of her minons slap me several times. I refuse to give her the crown. She cannot have the crown unless I give it freely. She cannot have it if I am dead, then it will revert to you."

"Is that her plan? To kill you and make me give her the crown?"Aine said. "What if I never give it to her, what if she kills you and then kills me, what happens to the crown?"

"Grianne knows if it's not given willingly she cannot wear it. It will be of no use to her. It will revert to a base metal, all magic gone from it." Her mom sighed. "And from faerie land, including her land Faeriedae." Her mom looked at her.

"Does Fennen know you are here?"

"No, not exactly." She told her mother what happened. "But, Patrick is on his way here and will be here in the morning. He may figure it out."

"But, the faerie world knows that Grianne has captured me?"

"Yes, according to Fennen, they continue to look for you."

"Then all hope is not lost," she said laying her head against Aine's. "There is hope yet."

10

The door banged open startling both Aine and her mother. Grianne smiled at them.

"Is the homecoming session over, ladies?" She rubbed her hands together. "Time to go, the faerie land is abuzz with the news of your capture, Fiona." She stared at Aine. "No one knows you are missing yet, Aine." She crooked her finger at them. "I believe that the CIF is close on your heels, Fiona. The Orrlaleigh swarm overhead but are not allowed in my lands."

"Who are the Orrlaleigh?" Aine asked.

Grianne sneered at Aine's mother. "Have you taught your daughter nothing about her heritage?" She turned to Aine and spoke as if she spoke to a child. "Orrlaleigh is the land of the flower faeries, the singing faeries, you know all the boring faeries. The land that your mother governs, or did." She gestured to two smaller dark faeries who came into the room. "Bring them to the throne room. Now!" The faeries hauled Aine and her mother up. Her mother appeared to be unsteady on her feet. Aine reached toward her but one of the faeries jerked her away. Grianne's faeries marched them out of the room down a forest path to another clearing. There, in the middle of the clearing stood a tall jeweled chair and Grianne leaped onto it. As soon as she sat down several smaller faeries put a green and brown cloak made of leaves over her shoulders. A crown of leaves adorned her head. One of the faeries handed her a crown of gold that shimmered in the dim light. It lay on a pillow of green velvet.

"That's my crown," her mother said.

"Not much longer," Grianne said. She crooked her finger again and faeries pushed Aine forward toward her.

"Now then," Grianne said. "I have a proposition for you. Either you give me the crown willingly or I kill your daughter. Simple and clean. Your choice, Fiona."

"You will never wear my crown, Grianne," her mother said. Grianne scowled at her.

"Then, you have made your choice," she said. She gestured to the faeries who held Aine. One of the faeries bent Aine's arm back and she screamed in pain. It felt like her arm split into two pieces. She bit her lip so hard she . The faerie pushed her down so that she knelt in the leaves. He held her arm behind her.

"Leave her alone," her mother said. Aine shook her head.

"I'm okay, Mom, don't give her the crown. No matter what she does." Aine closed her eyes in pain. Her arm ached. She smelled something hot. She opened her eyes as another faerie walked toward her smiling. In her hands she held a branding iron glowing red at the tip.

"Please, stop," her mother said. She appeared to be getting weaker. The faerie with the branding iron came close to Aine brandishing the iron near her face.

"A nice scar to remind you how you mother didn't save you," Grianne said. She gestured to the faerie who laid the tip against Aine's cheek. Aine screamed. The white burning searing pain flowed through her beginning at her cheek then traveling down her neck. All of her pain receptors fired at once. The smell of burning flesh reached her nostrils. She retched. She felt as if her body did not belong to herself. She floated above herself staring down at the faerie holding the branding iron to her face. She stepped away and Aine fell to one side moaning. She began to moan louder, the moaning turned into a song. A song filled with pain, longing and sorrow. The faerie holding the branding iron dropped the iron so that it bounced in the leaves. It hit a small puddle hissing as it cooled. Aine stood up with resolve in her eyes. Her mother watched her with wide eyes. The pain receded into a box in her mind. She shut the box holding the pain inside. She raised her hands to the sky and sang. All of the dark faeries held their hands to their ears.

"Stop that wailing," Grianne yelled. "Shut her up," she commanded. But, the faeries writhed on the ground clearly in pain as Aine sang note after note. The faeries that held her mother also let go and her mother ran over to her. She waved her mother away as she continued to sing. Her mother ran to Grianne and snatched the crown from the pillow. Grianne held her hands over her ears too but she took them off as Fiona grabbed the crown. She tried to take the crown back but Aine sang louder and Grianne grimaced

screaming as she put her hands to her ears
again.

Once her mother had the crown she
placed it on her head. A golden light
surrounded her illuminating the dark forest.
Suddenly, flower faeries swarmed in—Aine
thought they were the Orrlaleigh---lifting
her mother up past the tops of the trees until
Aine could no longer see her. She continued
to sing as the dark faeries scattered to get
away from her voice. But the louder she
sang, the more her voice carried. She felt as
if her voice reached around the world. She
felt her body rise with each note she sang.
She rose to the tops of the trees where
sunlight streamed in. Lifting her feet she
leaped toward the sunlight. She stopped
singing. Her cheek burned. Hands carried
her higher and higher until she soared free of
the treetops. Surrounded by flower faeries of
all colours they flew her above the dark
forest. She expected to see the Lough Gur
beneath her but realized she must still be in
Faeriedae. The forest began to lighten, more
clearings visible below. Sunlight touched
her face. The faeries brought her down to a
field filled with purple and blue flowers.
Blue forget-me-nots, purple gillyflowers,

blue-eyed grass, purple Butterwort, and Bellflowers; bluebells; purple Butterfly bushes, Harebell, Honesty and blue Love-in-a-Mist. The faeries laid Aine down softly. The heady scent of the flowers enveloped her senses making her dizzy. She closed her eyes trying not to notice that her cheek burned with searing pain. She raised a hand to touch it but another hand held it back.

"No, don't touch it, Aine," Patrick said. She opened her eyes not sure who bent over her.

"Patrick?" she asked.

"I'm here, Aine. Lay still the healing faeries will bring some Sea Lettuce to lay on your cheek. It'll take the stinging away. I'm so sorry I didn't get there in time to save you from Grianne."

"It's okay, Patrick. Mother is safe, I am safe."

"Drink this, it's made from Dewberries and Moon cherries with some faerie magic infused in it." He cradled her head in his hands lifting it so she could drink from the golden goblet. She drank and laid her head back down. The pain eased a little.

"Thanks," she said beginning to slur her words. The drink made her sleepy.

"Where is Mother?" she asked.

"She's rallying the Orrlaleigh to attack Grianne for kidnapping her and hurting you."

"What will happen to Grianne?" Aine asked. Her thoughts were encased in cotton. A flower faerie came to her side. Dilly smiled at Aine and laid a cool substance on her cheek.

"That should make it feel better, "Dilly said. "I'm afraid there will be a scar but it'll be small."

"Thanks," Aine mumbled. She closed her eyes taking in the scent of the flowers surrounding her. The murmuring of Patrick and Dilly's voices above her lulled her to sleep.

She awoke in a room. Her bedroom in her house. She sat up then laid back down. The room spun. Fennen walked in without knocking. He grinned at her.

"Up? I made tea and scones with real clotted cream. Come on," he came over to the side of the bed. Aine glanced down to make sure she had clothes on. Someone had dressed her in her oversized University of Michigan dorm shirt that reached to her knees. She sat up slower. She touched her cheek. It no longer hurt but she felt a small scar. It appeared to be healed. She slipped her feet into slippers and padded into the bathroom shutting the door before Fennen could follow her. She inspected her face in the mirror. Right below her left eye she saw a tiny scar, barely visible. She traced it with a fingertip. *I am branded by the dark faeries.* What does that mean? She came out almost running into Fennen.

"I'm hungry, Fen, where's my breakfast?"

"That's my girl, come on."

Her mom bustled around the kitchen. Aine ran over to her and embracing her from behind.

"Mom! You're safe!"

"Of course I'm safe. Fennen made us breakfast, sit down and I'll pour you tea." Patrick came out of the guest bedroom looking sleepy.

"Patrick!" Aine ran over to him embracing him too.

"Hey, I didn't get a hug," Fennen said pouting. Aine smiled leaving Patrick to hug Fennen.

"Let's sit down before the scones get cold," her mother said. Aine sat down. Patrick sat on one side of her, Fennen on the other side.

"What happened to Grianne?" Aine asked taking a bite of a scone. The buttery goodness melted in her mouth.

"She's still Queen of the Dark Faeries," Patrick answered. "But, she won't be bothering you again. At least we hope she won't."

Fennen looked at Aine. "You can barely see the scar," he said reaching out to touch Aine's cheek. She pulled away.

"Don't touch me," she said.

Her mom looked at her. Aine looked down. She wished everyone would stop looking at her.

"I didn't know you had the gift of song, called Giefu Saggws.."

"I can incapacitate dark faeries just by singing?"

"So it appears," her mother said taking a drink of her tea.

Aine touched her cheek rubbing the scar. "It doesn't hurt anymore."

Patrick took her hand in his. "I'm glad you are here," he said.

"How did you find me?" she asked taking another bite of her scone.

"The seals told me where you were. I'm sorry I didn't get there in time."

"It's fine, at least you made it." He took her hand up to his mouth and kissed it.

"If you still want me, Aine. I still want to marry you." He reached in his pocket and pulled out a ring.

"I'd be honored if you'd wear this sometimes." He held out an old-fashioned band etched with Celtic designs. She held it in her hand. The heat from her hand caused an engraving to appear. "Is breá liom tú," she read aloud. She looked at Patrick and translated it. "I love you," she said. On the inside were her and Patrick's initials intertwined. She placed the ring on her right ring finger. "I will wear it," she said. "But, I don't want to be engaged. I want to be free to date other guys. I'm too young to be tied down," she said admiring the ring.

"Then, I still have a chance?" Fennen asked taking her other hand in his. Both of them held one hand. She looked from one to the other then at her mom in desperation.

"Mom, help me," Aine asked.

The ringing of the phone interrupted them. Fennen jumped up to answer it. He held it out to Aine.

"It's for you," he said sitting back down scooting his stool closer to her. Patrick did the same thing.

"Hello?"

"Hey, Aine, where ya been? You missed a couple of days of school," Jess said. "You okay? I tried your cell but your Voice Mail came on."

"I'm okay, Jess, thanks. Just had a small accident, I cut my cheek but I'm all right. I fell against my dresser and hit my head too. I have a concussion so my mom made me stay home for a couple of days."

"You up for a movie night? Sarah is coming over. We were going to invite that new girl, Grace? But, I guess she left. Rumor is she transferred again."

"Yeah, I think that's what happened," Aine said. She got up away from the two boy faeries. Smiling she said, "I'd love to do a movie night with the girls." At that moment Dilly flew into the room. "Can I bring a friend? I met this new girl and she's anxious to meet other people."

"Sure, bring her along. We're meeting at Sarah's at seven. I'm making brownies with chocolate frosting. You can bring something too. Sarah will make popcorn and soda."

"Great, see you then." She hung up smiling at Dilly.

"Want to come with me to Sarah's tonight?" she asked. "You can only come if you promise to use your faerie glamour to hide your wings. Sarah and Jess don't know about faeries."

Dilly smiled. She blinked and her wings disappeared. She looked like a tiny teenage girl with long blonde hair standing in the kitchen.

"Like this?" Dilly asked.

"Exactly like that," Aine said. "Now if you'll excuse me I'm going to get dressed." She turned to Patrick and Fennen. "And, I don't want to see either of you when I come back out. Understand?"

Both boys nodded. Aine went into her bedroom to get dressed. Dilly followed her. She lay on the bed as Aine pulled on jeans and one of her favourite tee shirts, the one with the Tardis on it.

"Thanks for inviting me tonight," Dilly said. "Your mother is sending Fennen back to Ireland. She said the danger is over." She smiled. "But, she said I could stay. I get to have the guest room."

"Are you my bodyguard?" Aine asked brushing her hair. Or trying to. She gave up and bunched it up with a hair tie.

"In a way, I guess."

"I'm okay with that as long as you keep your wings hidden. Are you coming to school with me again?"

"Yes, only I'll come as a transfer student. It'll be easier to only use a little glamour to hide my wings rather than use a lot of glamour to hide my whole self."

Aine smiled. She went into the bathroom and used makeup foundation to cover the scar. It blended in so only a faint line appeared. "Gives me character," Aine said to her image.

Dilly left the bedroom before Aine came out. Aine fingered the ring Patrick had given her. She took it off holding it in the palm of her hand until the letters reappeared. *Two years*. She took the ring off and put it in her jewelry box. Grabbing her jeans jacket she headed out the door.   ###

ABOUT THE AUTHOR

Kathleen began writing at the age
of eight when she self-published a
book of poetry. She has been
writing ever since. She writes in
different genres but Young Adult
fantasy is her favourite.
Find out more information:
Website: www.gaelicfairie.webs.com
On Twitter as: @kathleea
On Facebook as: Witch Hunter
Book Trailers on YouTube.com
Find her books on most online
retailers and in bookstores.

Kathleen S. Allen

Made in the USA
Charleston, SC
31 May 2011